PRAISE FOR UNQUIET FOREST!

"THIS. WAS. AMAZING. With 47 books read this year so far, this is my standout favorite. Juliet weaves a tale of quiet horror that keeps you reading. I am a slow reader. I went through this fast. I couldn't wait for the next chapter." Brýn Grover, Beyond the Pale

***

"UNQUIET FOREST is a one-of-a-kind ghost story full of anger and generational trauma. Even the forest isn't safe from the echoes of evil." Wayne Turmel, Johnny Lycan: Werewolf PI series.

***

"Juliet Rose creates an eerie atmosphere with the creepy woods and an abandoned asylum, while also shedding light on the mistreatment of people with disabilities in such institutions. It's haunting, immersive, and deeply impactful—a must-read for fans of atmospheric horror with heart." Kati Chastain, 27 Bones, pt II

***

"I generally lean towards extreme horror, but THIS is the first book I've read this year, out of 41, that has given me nightmares. It really got in my head, and I loved every single moment of it. No spoilers from me. But trust me, you want to read this." Shaina Mangum, Shots by Shai

***

"This is a beautiful story about courage and friendship in the face of terror and cruelty. The vivid descriptions of the lush forest made me feel like I was there." Stephanie Huddle

***

"This is one of the best books I've read so far this year. Easily. If you're a fan of quiet horror, ghosts, and your emotions being played with - this is the one." Danielle's Madhouse Reviews & Services

Unquiet Forest

Juliet Rose

ABOVE THE RAIN COLLECTIVE

Above the Rain Collective

abovetheraincollective@gmail.com

North Georgia, USA

Contributing Editor: J.A. Sexton

Publisher's note:

This is a work of fiction. All characters and incidents are the product of the author's imagination, places are used fictitiously and any resemblance to an actual person, living or dead, is entirely coincidental.

ISBN: 979-8-9899186-8-3

First Printing June 2025

abovetheraincollective.com

Cover graphics and interior formatting by J.A. Sexton

Original cover photos from Pixabay

Above the Rain Collective logo artwork by Bee Freitag

CONTENTS

***

For Louise

***

FOREWORD

There are authors and then there is Juliet Rose. Not only is Juliet an award-winning author of over sixty awards, a publisher, and a mass supporter of other authors, but she is also a very talented multi-genre writer. Her work spans everything from contemporary, disability fiction, addiction fiction, folklore, time travel, social justice, action and adventure, horror, and everything in between.

As a horror author, I can say her scary stories are some of the best quiet horror. I love Through the Surface and By the Dimming Light as they touch on different aspects of ghastly spookiness and the human condition, but with Unquiet Forest, Rose takes it a step further. She pushes a narrative full of twists, turns, and wonder. What starts as troubled teens in the forest quickly becomes an unsettling mystery of terror, the supernatural, and humanity's dark past. Unquiet Forest asks difficult questions with even tougher answers. Juliet paints a beautiful portrayal of loss, love, and decay.

Not only is this one of the best supernatural ghost stories of the year, but it's a truly riveting spookfest with loads of layers, heart, and soul. With each release, Juliet gets better and better, with this one being no different. Unquiet Forest may be Rose's best horror work to date and is worthy of the big screen. I want to see this as a movie!

DZ Hollow

PROLOGUE

"Let it burn!" the old woman screamed as she was being dragged away by police. "Let it burn!"

The police paid her no mind as they escorted her to the ambulance and handed her off to the waiting paramedics. The woman tried to break free, but she was too weak, and they strapped her to the gurney to prevent her from escaping. She clawed at the young female paramedic and forced her to meet her eyes. "Honey, you must listen to me. It will keep happening until the building is burned."

The thin, twenty-something paramedic patted her hand and smiled. "It's okay now. They have removed everyone from the building, and it will be shut down. No one else will be hurt in there."

The older woman's eyes fixed on the window of the door, her mouth in a downturned grimace. "You don't understand. That structure holds things, bad things."

"No, they have arrested those who were breaking the law.

3

The state is shutting the institution down for good. It's over," the paramedic assured the old woman, who reminded her of her own grandmother. "Did you work there?"

The old woman began to tear up and shook her head in defeat. "No."

"Oh, were you one of the residents?"

"No. I came to help."

"Well, that was nice of you. I'm sure they appreciated that. What's your name?"

"Margaret. Margaret Blankenship," the old woman muttered to herself.

The paramedic patted her again and smiled. "Nice to meet you, Margaret. I'm Judy."

The woman didn't respond. Judy checked her vitals, and other than seeming weak and disoriented, with burns from the fire she'd started, Margaret seemed to be in good health. The ambulance started up as the other paramedic, Gary, eased it out and down the dirt road. The institution was in an isolated spot, people said it was because crazies lived there, but all they found were dead and emaciated children and adults, mostly disabled. Strangely, only a few of the staff were around. There were a mere handful listed on the staff roster. Not nearly enough to run an institution of that size. Margaret wasn't on the staff roster or list of residents, and she was covered with burns all over her hands and arms.

Margaret was found in the basement with a raging fire. She tried to stop them from putting it out, but the fire department extinguished it immediately. She screamed and fought them; however, she was frail, and they were able to remove her from the premises. Her and about seven surviving residents. The rest were found chained to their beds, sinks, and pipes, starved to death.

No one in the nearby town, which was over thirty miles away, knew much about the place except it was listed as an institution for the invalid. Mentally and physically disabled.

No one knew anyone who worked there. Or about any of the residents. Odd, but that's just how it was.

Judy leaned forward to talk to the ambulance driver, Gary, her voice low. "Have you ever seen anything like it?"

"No. That was some freaky shit. Who called it in?" he replied, keeping his eyes on the thin, overgrown road.

"I don't know. The call came from the facility, but when they got there, only Margaret was around, and she didn't make the call."

"How do you know?"

"Well, first, they said it was like a man's voice. Deep, gravelly, hard to understand. Second, she didn't want the firefighters to stop her from burning the place down," Judy answered, glancing back at the old woman.

"Where did they find the remaining staff?"

"That was strange, too. They were huddled together on their knees in a room on the second floor and were chanting, all facing the same direction. The police said they didn't seem to know where they were. They didn't want to leave."

"Huh. This is all pretty horrifying if you ask me," Gary muttered, keeping his eye on the road as the ambulance bounced over the rough terrain. He shook his head. "Weird, the road seems longer and more narrow than when we came in this way."

Judy didn't reply as she'd sat back to check on Margaret, who'd fallen silent. Judy gasped and put her hand on Gary's shoulder. He frowned and glanced back, seeing Judy leaning over the old woman, checking her vitals.

"She alright?"

Judy shook her head, her eyes round. "She's dead."

CHAPTER 1

T he teens filtered out of their delivering vehicles and came to a clump in the center of the parking field. None making eye contact with the others, yet ever-watchful of their future companions. There were eight in total gathered in the haphazard group, ages thirteen to fifteen. Older teens were assigned to a different group. Each of them had their hiking and camping gear at their feet as they tried in vain to get the internet on their phones.

"Won't do you any good," a loud voice from behind them said as one of their assigned adult leaders made his way over to the group. "No service out here. Using good old-fashioned CB radios from here on out. I'm Craig, I'll be one of your guides for this little adventure."

The youngest ward, a girl of only thirteen, with shoulder-length, light-brown hair and green eyes, spoke up. "Um, sir, how will we know things? You know, like where to go and stuff?"

At this, Craig laughed and shook his head, his long brown hair in a single braid twisting down his back. "What do you think people did back in the day without cell phones? We have a map, a compass, and a radio. I have also done this trail a hundred times. We'll be fine. Alright, I need you all to come close and when I call your name and age, please step over to my left, your right."

He gestured to the spot he meant, and the group glanced warily in that direction. The vehicles belonging to the parents and other adults who'd dropped the teens off began to drive away as they saw the children were now in the care of a responsible adult. They seemed in a hurry to leave and let the kids be someone else's problem for a bit.

Craig pulled out a clipboard and squinted down at it. "Danny Henry, fourteen?"

A skinny, short boy stepped forward, his black hair falling over his deep brown eyes. He slung his pack over his bony shoulder and moved to the open spot where they were supposed to regather. "Uh, sir? It's Hernandez."

Craig eyed him, then looked back at the list. "Oh, yeah, Hernandez, right."

"Brandi Masters, fifteen?"

A golden-blond-haired girl, with painted nails and full, ruby lips, looking more like twenty years old than a teenager, raised her hand and sighed. She didn't move. Craig frowned at her. "Do you have a question there, princess?"

"Yeah, aren't I a little old for this group?"

Craig chuckled dryly and stared at her. "You're here, aren't ya? I assume you are Brandi Masters, then. Go on and join Danny over there."

Brandi groaned and snatched her bag off the ground as she made her way to where Danny was standing. Craig watched for a moment before continuing on the list. "Let's save any questions for later, we need to get a move on to use the light. Chase Benson, thirteen. Jack Foley, fourteen.

Cara Adair, fourteen. Donita Pauley, fourteen. Junior, fifteen. What's your last name, Junior? It's smudged here."

A large boy with rich brown skin shifted his pack and spoke softly. "James."

"Junior James? Got it," Craig replied, adding a note to the list.

The girl who'd spoken initially to Craig picked up her pack and glanced at Craig. She was petite with a freckled face, making her look even younger than her age. "You didn't call my name. Magpie Abernathy?"

A few of the other kids snickered at her name, but Craig silenced them with a sharp look. He peered at his list and scribbled her name down. "Sorry, they forgot to put you on here. Seems about right. Right hand doesn't know what the left hand is doing. Your age?"

"Thirteen."

The rest of the teens shifted over to the new, but not any different, spot. Craig glanced at his watch and frowned, peering down the road leading to where they were. He stepped away and used the radio to make a call. The teens glanced at one another when Jack, a boy with light-blond hair, blue-gray eyes, and a mischievous grin, stared at Magpie.

"Is that your real name?" he asked.

She shrugged. "Is Jack your real name?"

He blushed and grunted. "Jack's a normal name, Magpie is a fucking bird."

Not one to be shut down, Magpie glared at him and stuck her chin in the air. "You look like a fucking bird with that chicken head."

At this, the rest of the group busted out laughing at his expense and began to loosen up. Jack looked away, his face turning red, but he laughed at what she said, even so. Craig came back over, his face twisted with concern. Something seemed off as he addressed the group.

"Okay, we need to hold up a minute. Our other guide,

Katie, was in an accident on her way, it seems. We're required to have two guides, a male and a female, since we're a co-ed group. They're sending someone else to join us in her place."

The teens stared at Craig for further instruction. Brandi pulled her phone out again and sighed loudly when it didn't have service. She rolled her eyes and placed her hand on her hip in a dramatic fashion.

Craig shook his head. "Again, like I said before, no service out here."

"Then why did we even bring them?" Junior asked.

Craig raised his eyebrows. "No one told you to bring phones."

Which was true, yet the teens had them. A product of their daily reality. A cell phone was the equivalent of bringing clothing. Not a want, a need. Except for Magpie. She didn't bring one, nor did she own one. She sat on the ground next to her pack and pulled out a sandwich she'd packed. The other teens followed her lead, and before long, they were sitting on a lopsided circle, munching on snacks they'd brought with them. Craig stepped away to try the radio again.

Chase, a stout boy with a round, serious face and auburn hair, spoke up. "Why are you all here?"

Jack jumped in a little too eagerly. "Stole a car."

"Slept with my teacher," Brandi added, almost seeming to try and one-up Jack.

The other kids stared in amazement at her for a moment before Magpie asked, "How are you here for that? Shouldn't your teacher be in trouble and not you?"

Brandi snorted. "Dear child, that's not how it works. I was labeled a 'seductress' and he was made out to be the victim. Poor school teacher manipulated by a bad girl. They told my parents I'd end up prostituting if they didn't send me here."

Magpie tipped her head. "That doesn't make any sense."

"And, yet, here I am," Brandi stated with a flick of her wrist.

Donita spoke next. "Got in a group fight at school."

"What's a group fight?" Chase questioned.

Donita shrugged. "What does it sound like? Like thirty of us got in a fight in the cafeteria."

"Did they get in trouble, too?" Magpie chimed in.

Donita smiled, brushing her thick, dark brown hair off her shoulder. "A little. Most suspensions. I got sent here because I organized the fight. They called me a gang leader."

"Are you?" Chase asked, his eyes fixed on her face.

"A gang leader? Nah. Not in that way. Yeah, I got everyone to go along, but not for any devious reason. Just a pissed-off bitch, I guess."

Magpie stared at her in awe. "Why'd you do it, then?"

"I was bored."

Cara smiled, her golden eyes soulful, as she twisted a strand of chestnut hair with highlights between her fingers. "Shoplifting. I didn't need the stuff, but we were all doing it. Makeup, jewelry, things like that."

They fell silent for a moment. Junior cleared his throat. "I actually didn't do shit. They blamed me for no reason. Just because of how I look."

"What do you mean?" Brandi asked.

"Look at me, why do you think?" They all did. Junior was a large, black kid with a goofy smile and hard but kind eyes. He appeared intimidating until he spoke. "They said I broke into a pharmacy and stole some pills in my hometown. Said they had me on camera."

"Did you?" Brandi inquired, her voice soft.

"Nope. Was home in bed, but they didn't listen to me about that. I don't have time for that kinda stuff. I'm going to Harvard when I graduate."

The group laughed until they saw he was dead serious. Magpie tipped her head. "For what?"

"I'm going to be a doctor," Junior replied, his voice filled with pride and determination.

"Cool," Chase said, clearly impressed. "I tried to set the school on fire."

They all stared in disbelief. Chase looked like he would be the one who wanted to be a doctor. He ran his hand through his hair and grinned. "No shit. I failed my math test and knew my father would beat my ass over it, so I thought if I burned down the school, they wouldn't be able to see my grades."

Jack laughed and slapped the side of his thigh. "You know that shit's on the cloud, right? They can see it from anywhere."

Chase blushed but chuckled. "Yeah, I found that out later. But my dad was no longer pissed about my grades. Now he's pissed 'cause I'm a pyro."

"Pyro?" Magpie asked.

"Pyromaniac. Means he likes to burn stuff," Danny replied. They'd almost forgotten he was there. Danny, the short, thin boy, rubbed his bottom lip as he stared off. "My friends and I set off fireworks in the grocery store. On a dare."

For some reason, that didn't come as too much of a shock, even though he looked like he could be only eleven years old. Magpie shifted uneasily, hoping they'd glazed over her. However, Chase looked in her direction. "You?"

Magpie stared at the ground, not wanting to speak. Seeing they were going to wait until she did, she glanced back up. "Stabbed my grandpa. He isn't dead, though, just in the hospital."

This silenced the group. Most of them were there for minor crimes. Magpie was there for attempted murder. Donita cocked her head. "You're a little badass, aren't you?"

Magpie didn't have time to answer before Craig came back over. He seemed stressed and kept checking the radio, almost nervously. Maybe he didn't want to be alone with a bunch of teens. After about fifteen minutes, he called out to them. "Alright, let's gather up and get moving."

"I thought we were waiting for the other guide?" Junior asked.

Craig sighed, seeming distracted. "She'll have to catch up to us. We need to make it the first checkpoint before dark, or we'll get stuck on the trail without any light. She knows where that is. Grab your packs and let's go."

The teens glanced between them, not comfortable with the change in plans. However, being taught they needed to listen to authority, they formed a ragtag group and trailed behind Craig as he led them into the woods. The sounds of birds and the scurrying of small animals made it seem less daunting.

Magpie found Chase watching her and smiled at him. He quickly shifted his eyes away and didn't smile back. They were scared of her now. Scared of her willingness to take a knife to a family member. She was used to people holding her at arm's length. Not because of that, but because of her abilities. Something she almost never told anyone about. Her ability to see and talk to ghosts.

The other thing they didn't know and she didn't want to tell them was why she'd try to kill her grandfather. What horrible secrets lay between them.

If she didn't kill him, he was going to use her to open a door that couldn't be closed. To bring forth a power he'd been waiting on for years. One handed down in their family but restricted because of its potential to cause great harm.

One Magpie was determined to end once and for all.

CHAPTER 2

By the time the group made it to the first checkpoint to camp for the night, they were tired and cranky, picking at each other over every little thing. Some of the teens had paired off, chatting as they hiked. Mostly by age. Brandi and Junior, both fifteen, quickly separated themselves from the younger ones, even though the age difference was mere months in some cases. The chunk of the kids were fourteen but vastly different in maturity levels.

Donita and Cara paired off, walking quietly side by side. Jack and Danny trailed behind, cutting up and telling gross jokes. At first, Craig tried to stop them, but eventually gave up as his mind was elsewhere. This left Chase and Magpie, who awkwardly walked near each other but not together. Chase struggled with the amount of hiking and eventually ended up lagging behind. Out of courtesy, Magpie stuck with him.

"So, your parents really named you Magpie?" Chase asked, already knowing the answer. "After a bird?"

Magpie shrugged. "Your parents really named you Chase? After the verb?"

Chase turned red and chuckled. "Point."

Craig paused up ahead, glancing at his compass. He placed his hand over his brows and peered up the trail. Up. They were climbing a mountain to get to the first checkpoint. He gazed at the teens, his eyes staying perhaps for a moment too long on Brandi, then went on.

Junior shifted his pack and yelled forward. "Uh, sir? How much longer?"

Craig barely turned as he responded. "Almost there, and I'm not your father, so don't call me sir. It's Craig."

The kids wondered what timeline *almost there* meant to Craig, and after another hour of hiking, found out it was not what they were hoping. By nightfall, they'd made it to the first campsite, which to their relief had three rustic shelters. Not cabins, really. More like wooden tents. Even so, it meant they didn't have to sleep completely exposed in the North Georgia mountains. Craig showed the girls their structure and told the boys to take the one on the far side, as he took the one in between.

"Don't unpack anything. We're here to sleep and eat only. We'll be up before the sun rises to go on," he ordered.

Danny raised his hand, and Craig frowned at him, gesturing for the boy to speak. Danny glanced around. "Where are we supposed to get food?"

Craig shook his head. "What, you didn't pack any?"

The teens stared at one another, they hadn't been told to pack food. Just clothes and supplies. Craig waited a moment, then leaned back and laughed. "Had you there. In each structure is a pack. This has our food for the next twenty-four hours until we get to the following checkpoint. It also has basic medical supplies and toiletries."

"Toiletries?" Chase asked.

"You know, toothpaste and stuff."

"Oh. Who puts this stuff here?" Chase inquired.

"Wilderness Reset," Craig explained, growing agitated with the series of questions.

The company, Wilderness Reset, worked with the court systems and local law enforcement to take wayward youth out on nature expeditions to find themselves, and theoretically get off the bad path they were on. Supposedly, to put them in the direction to a better life. The flyer the teens were shown was cheesy and used nature analogies to describe the teens' experience, such as "turning wild saplings into strong trees" and weird stuff like that. Most parents jumped at the chance when it was presented. Especially because it was a program paid for by the state to offset future incarceration.

The teens split off into their spaces, setting their packs down and rooting through the provided supplies. It wasn't much, and it wasn't good. Canned ravioli, pears, containers of colored water pretending to be juice, crackers, and, for the morning, off-brand Pop-Tarts. In the pack were also sandwiches and bruised apples for them to take on their hike the following day. Wilderness Reset clearly spared no expense.

With no way to heat the food, they opened the cans with their multitools and ate the food cold. Magpie picked at hers, even though she was hungry. She could taste the chemicals in the processed ravioli, so she focused on pears and crackers. Chase wandered over, eyeing her leftover food.

"Are you going to eat that?" he asked, pointing at her can of ravioli.

Magpie shrugged and lifted the can to him. "You can have it."

He sat down next to her, his head cocked. "You aren't hungry?"

"I am, but this is garbage. I'd rather eat grass." She nibbled on a canned pear, relieved it was at least not super processed. She could still taste the metallic can on the fruit, but pushed past her distaste. "We don't eat like this at home."

"Oh yeah? What do you eat?"

"We have a garden, and my father hunts. I can hunt, too. We all can. My family doesn't believe in tainting our blood with commercial food, so we grow or hunt most of it. My grandpa goes into town once a month for dried goods like flour and beans."

"The grandfather you stabbed?" Chased asked, then blushed. "Sorry."

"Don't be. I did stab him," Magpie replied, nonchalantly.

"Did he, like, touch you or something?'

Magpie stared at Chase, not understanding, when it dawned on her what he was asking. "No, he wouldn't do anything like that."

"Then, why? Was he mean?" Chase pressed.

"My family is just different," Magpie answered, skirting the question.

Chase watched her, his eyes narrowed to try and figure out what would drive her to try and kill her own grandfather. "Different how?"

Magpie looked away. He wouldn't understand. For generations, her family had lived not far from where they were currently, staying away from society and hiding their dark secrets. Children weren't allowed to go to school and were strictly forbidden from talking about the family's special abilities. When Magpie was little and realized at least some of the people she interacted with throughout the day were no longer living, she asked her mother who they were and why she could see them. The response was simply that she had the "gift".

Not all of her family could talk to ghosts, however. Some were psychic, some had no special abilities beyond calling up the spirits, as they said. The spirits could be anything from dead people to dark entities. Entities they worked with to do unsavory things. Things Magpie wanted nothing to do with. Her grandpa was the oldest living member of their family and, therefore, the head.

Cut off the head and kill the beast.

She looked at Chase and shrugged. "Just weird."

He nodded. "Yeah, mine too. My grandma is addicted to diet soda and soap operas."

Magpie laughed, realizing she liked Chase. He was dorky and soft but genuine. She could read it in his soul. "You said you are a pyromaniac? You like to set stuff on fire?"

"Oh. Not really. Just that once, and clearly I wasn't very good at it," Chase replied with a grin. He finished off the can of ravioli and set it down.

"So, the school didn't burn down?"

"Nah. I set a fire, but the sprinkler system came on and put it out. They caught it all on the security camera. The school agreed not to press charges if I came here."

Magpie watched the other teens, who were also talking in small groups. She and Chase were the youngest, so the others seemed to want to separate themselves from the pair. Brandi's eyes were fixed on Junior, who was telling a story and waving his arms as the others around him laughed. Jack and Danny were whispering with their heads together, probably up to no good.

Magpie looked around for Craig and saw him in his structure, reading a book. He was turned so he could observe their campsite, however, his eyes seemed to be drawn to one thing. Brandi. Magpie didn't like the way Craig was watching her and thought about how Chase asked if her grandpa had touched her. He hadn't, but something inside told her that Craig wanted to touch Brandi.

She got up and walked over to Craig to break the trance. He glanced at her and frowned. "Yeah?"

"When is the other guide coming?"

Craig set his book down and sighed. "Hopefully, tonight. If not, first thing in the morning."

"Okay. Are we safe out here?" Magpie asked to keep him focused on her.

19

"Didn't you say you live out this way?" Craig replied. "Aren't you safe there?"

"Yes, but we have guns and a house to keep us safe." She also didn't mean the threat was the forest.

"Guns, eh? You can shoot?" Craig seemed genuinely interested.

"I can, but I don't have a gun on me," Magpie answered.

Craig grinned and patted his bag. "No, I imagine you don't. Good thing I do."

Magpie's eyes darted to the pack, then back to Craig. "Oh. I didn't know you were allowed to carry a gun on this trip."

He shrugged and picked his book back up. "Allowed, not allowed. We're in the wild. Anything else?"

She shook her head and wandered back to her sleeping bag. Chase had joined the larger group, and she was alone, which was good. She needed to be by herself to do what she had to do. She closed her eyes and took slow, deep breaths, shutting off the outside world. When she opened her eyes, she was joined by a young girl about her age. The girl was thin and pale, wearing tattered clothing.

Magpie smiled at her. "Hi."

The girl met Magpie's eyes, her own dishwater brown ones showing wisdom beyond her age. "Hello, I'm Amelia. Why am I here?"

"I'm Magpie. I need your help. See that man over there? His name is Craig. I have a bad feeling about him. Do you know anything about him?"

The girl got up and moved unseen across to Craig's structure. She approached him and passed through his body. As she came back out, she met Magpie's eyes and shook her head. She was back to Magpie's side in an instant and spoke.

"He isn't here for the right reasons. He is running from something and using this to hide from whatever that is," the girl explained simply.

"Will he hurt us?" Magpie asked for confirmation of what she had already read in his soul.

The girl looked back over at Craig. "He has desires he shouldn't have and secrets. He doesn't want to physically hurt you, but his desires could create harm. He is fighting two forces."

Magpie gazed at the gathered teens. Jack and Danny were now with them, as well, as they laughed and told stories. "What about any of them?"

The girl followed Magpie's gaze and disappeared. A moment later, she was back. "They mean no harm. Some are misunderstood. Some are unloved. None are mean-spirited."

Magpie smiled. She had gathered the same. "Thank you for your help. Do you want to play a game with me since you are here now, Amelia?"

The girl smiled and nodded. Magpie raised her hands and they began to play games of patty-cake and cat's cradle with invisible yarn. As the teens returned to their structures to bed down, the girl vanished. Magpie climbed into her sleeping bag and watched the others do the same. She glanced at Craig, and a feeling she couldn't shake overtook her.

He wouldn't survive this journey.

CHAPTER 3

T he following morning, before the sun crept into the sky, Craig woke everyone up to get ready for the next segment of their experience. After a lot of groans and complaints, the teens took turns relieving themselves and changing their clothes. Craig pointed out they wouldn't be able to properly bathe or wash their clothes for a week, so not to blow through the small amount of clothes they'd packed for the journey. He was wearing the same outfit from the day before.

At this, Brandi wrinkled her nose in disgust. "I'm not wearing the same clothes for two days."

Craig laughed. "Either way, if you change every day, you'll end up wearing those clothes again. How many days' worth of clothes do you have with you?"

Brandi frowned and mentally calculated. "Two more after today."

"And we have five more days of hiking before we get to the first place we can take showers and wash clothes."

An incredible look of revulsion passed over Brandi's face, and she made a noise that sounded like a trapped animal. "That's cruel and unusual punishment! You can't expect us to live like this. We have the right to clean clothes."

Craig turned serious, his eyes tired but firm. "You gave up your rights when you got yourself sent here. If you don't like it, you shouldn't have screwed up."

"Screwed being the operative word," Jack interjected with a smirk.

Danny began to laugh when Craig cut his eyes at him. "This isn't funny. You kids put yourselves here with your irresponsible actions. Sorry if you don't like it, but too bad," he growled, showing a side of himself they hadn't seen yet. Though Magpie had sensed it from the beginning.

Something about their guide was just off.

"Where is the other guide?" Magpie asked. "You said she'd be here by this morning."

"Well, she's not, now, is she? I'm in charge, you aren't, so stop asking stupid questions. Get your stuff together and let's get moving," Craig ordered.

"What about breakfast?" Chase asked.

Craig whipped around, glaring at Chase, who took a step back. Craig pointed to the packs in the structure. "Did you eat the pastries sealed in the silver foil?"

"Uh, no," Chase replied, his ears turning red.

"Then grab them and you can eat as we hike. We don't have time to waste."

Not one to be deterred, Magpie stood her ground. "We can't go without the other guide. We are supposed to have a male and female guide for our safety. I think we should wait for her here."

Craig eyed her, his face like stone. "She isn't coming. So move your little ass."

Magpie didn't like how he was speaking to her, and a flash of warning crossed her mind. He knew all along there wouldn't be another guide. He'd been lying to them from the moment they'd arrived. For what purpose? Why had he kept checking the radio if the other guide wasn't coming? There was more going on than he was telling them, and this set off alarms in Magpie.

"Shouldn't we stay here, or go back to where we were dropped off?"

"With what food? Are you planning to starve? We need to go to the next checkpoint to get more supplies, including the next allotment of food. Going back only shorts us even more since everyone has gone from there. That's simply a drop-off point," Craig countered, saying it as a command and not an option.

"What about the radio? Can't you call for help? Have someone meet us?" Magpie insisted, feeling she was losing ground.

"I could, but I won't. Remember, child, you do what I tell you. Got it?"

"I will report this," Magpie said, her voice low and controlled.

Craig shrugged. "Yeah, whatever. Get your shit and let's go."

His use of curse words surprised all of them, and they glanced amongst themselves. This was quickly shifting into something they weren't expecting. Instead of the camp counselor type person they were expecting, Craig was proving to be no different than the police. Magpie wanted to fight back, but the spirits were telling her otherwise. At least, for now. She gathered her pack and waited until the group began to walk before following. Chase fell in with her, eating a crumbling toaster pastry that made her want to vomit.

"You okay?" he asked between bites.

"Yeah, why?"

"Oh, that was weird back there, right? Craig, I mean?" he said, his eyes darting to Craig's back up ahead.

Magpie peered up at the shifting form of their guide. "I suppose. Something felt off about him from the beginning, though, don't you think? He seemed to be hiding something."

Chase cocked his head, considering. "I don't know. All adults seem off to me."

"I guess, but this is something different than that. He is acting odd."

"You don't think he's leading us into the middle of nowhere to murder us, do you?" Chase joked.

Joke or not, Magpie didn't trust their appointed leader. "I wouldn't put it past him."

Thinking she was kidding, Chase snickered and finished the last bits of the pastry. They fell silent and pushed forward as the day wore on. Around midday, they stopped and ate the provided sandwiches. Peanut butter, not even with jelly. The apples tasted like sponges, and the sandwiches had the essence of growing mold. Magpie ate only what she needed to not pass out and hoped they'd encounter some type of berry bushes or fruit trees.

Craig tried less and less to hide his true intent and more than once, Magpie caught him leering at Brandi, staring at her chest with a creepy smile. Figuring she knew the forest as well as he probably did, Magpie hatched a plan to run away in the night to find help. Maybe she could convince the others to go with her.

It was dark by the time they made it to the next checkpoint, and the teens were disappointed to find more of the same stale food left behind for them. Wherever the money went to have them there, it certainly wasn't going to food or supplies.

Cara seemed to not be feeling well and lay down without eating. Magpie worried if they didn't get help, Cara might become seriously sick and considered talking to Craig. However, after their previous encounter, she knew he had no desire to make things easier on them. She wanted to talk to the other kids, but Craig seemed to head her off at any chance she got to be alone with them. By the time they bedded down, Cara looked worse for wear and seemed to be running a light fever. She shivered uncontrollably in the warm night air.

Once Magpie was sure Craig was asleep, it was after midnight, and Cara was tossing and turning in her sleep. Magpie went to wake Donita and Brandi, however, Brandi wasn't in her sleeping bag. Magpie crept out of the structure and scanned around the campsite. Craig was missing from his structure, as well. A voice whispered to check the woods, but she didn't want to confront Craig alone, so Magpie went and woke Junior, the largest of them.

Junior rolled over, his eyes confused with sleep. "Hey, what's up?"

"Brandi is missing. So is Craig," Magpie whispered, trying to not wake the others.

His eyes immediately cleared, and he sat up. "Damn. I've seen him eyeing her. Do you know where they went?"

"No, but something is telling me to go check in the forest," Magpie said, not letting him know *something* was most definitely a spirit. "Will you go with me to find them?"

"Yeah, let me get my shoes on. Hold on." Junior sat up and fished around in the dark for his shoes.

Once he was ready, Magpie led the way, following her instinct and guides. They wound through the trees toward an outcropping. As they approached the stone overhang, they could make out two figures, one grabbing the other. Junior put his finger to his lips as they crouched behind a fallen tree. They could make out Craig with his hands grasping Brandi by the upper arms. She looked scared, even though she was trying to hide it.

"Let me go, Craig. I need to get back to bed."

"In time. You know you like this. I mean, you like older men, after all, right? Ones in positions of authority. You want this as much as I do, so stop fighting," Craig coaxed like a snake luring its prey.

They could see Brandi was trying to keep control of the situation, but was rapidly losing the battle. Even though she was brash, she was still only a teenage girl. Craig was larger than her and willing to do whatever it took to get what he wanted. Brandi tried to squirm away.

"I'll scream if you don't stop," she bargained, her eyes darting around for an escape.

"Who will hear you? Those other delinquents back there? They don't care. No one cares about kids like you. They wouldn't believe you anyway because this is your MO, right?"

"MO?" Brandi asked, trying to stall.

"Modus Operandi. You are a whore. You'll always be a whore. So, stop resisting and let's get this over with. I won't tell if you won't," he replied, his words dripping with sarcasm.

Brandi yanked away, and Craig reached out and slapped her across the face. Her eyes grew wide with shock at the strike. She was trapped and knew it. He was going to rape her and no one would believe her. *If* he let her live, which was quickly looking like a slim possibility as he pushed her closer to the edge.

Junior and Magpie glanced at each other, comprehending the seriousness of the situation. Craig had every intent to cause harm if it got him what he was after. They, too, could see Brandi would likely not make it out alive after Craig raped her. Magpie tuned into the spirits and asked for guidance. The only thing that came back to her mind was the word *fight*.

As if he heard it as well, Junior began to stand up. At that moment, Craig let one of his hands drop to his shorts to unbuckle them, and Junior took his chance. He began to run full speed at the pair, yelling at the top of his lungs. Magpie was on his heels and hoped they could save Brandi in time.

The noise startled Craig, who let Brandi go and whipped around to see where it was coming from. Brandi bolted out of the way as Junior barreled down on the shocked guide. Craig went to put his hands up to block Junior, but the burly and angry teen hit Craig full force, sending him flying over the edge of the outcropping.

Junior's feet slid as he tried to stop himself before tumbling over the ledge, as well. He almost went over when Brandi lunged forward and grabbed his arm, giving him enough pull back to stop. Rocks and dirt tumbled over in his place. Brandi wrapped her arms around Junior and began to cry. Magpie stood off to the side, her heart racing. She crept to the edge and peered down, however, it was too dark to see anything.

Junior and Brandi came up beside her and glanced over. Brandi had a flashlight and shone it down, but the light disappeared into the abyss. She frowned. "Do you think he's dead?"

Magpie closed her eyes and listened inside, receiving the answer she was hoping to hear in response. "Yes."

Junior rubbed his face and turned to them. "I hope you're right, or he's going to be pissed."

Magpie smiled to herself. Craig was most definitely dead.

CHAPTER 4

T he three stood staring over the ledge, trying to decide what to do next. Despite Craig trying to hurt Brandi, killing him was still a crime, and they were already there for breaking the law. At least, most of them were. Junior rubbed his face with his broad hand, his eyes wide as the reality of the situation sank in.

"I'm going to go to prison," he muttered.

"No, you won't! He was going to rape me. Kill me, maybe even," Brandi countered brashly. "Besides, no one but us three knows what happened out here. We should just go back to camp and say nothing about it. Pretend like it didn't happen."

"Uh, won't they notice Craig's missing?" Junior replied, pointing out the flaw in the plan.

"We can just say we woke up and he was gone," Magpie chimed in. "That, like, he went to relieve himself. We can help look for him in the morning and say we found him and he fell over the cliff or something."

"This far from camp?" Junior asked.

That was a good point. Magpie shrugged. "I don't know. I think we play dumb. Make a pact to never say anything to anyone. Not even the other kids."

Brandi nodded. "I'm down."

Junior glanced between the two of them and chewed his lip. "Okay. Swear?"

"Swear," Magpie answered, more than happy to get rid of Craig once and for all.

"Me too. I swear," Brandi whispered. "We should get back to the camp before anyone else notices us missing and comes looking for us."

The three of them crept back through the forest, careful to be silent so they didn't wake the others. Junior went into the boys' structure first and gave them a thumbs-up as he slipped in, the other boys still sound asleep.

Brandi and Magpie went to their structure and climbed in. Donita sat up, rubbing her eyes. "Hey. Was wondering where you went."

"Had to pee," Magpie offered.

"Together?" Donita asked, though she didn't seem to really care.

Brandi slipped into her sleeping bag. "Passed each other on the way, so I waited to make sure Magpie made it back safely."

Donita lay back down and yawned. "Oh, hey, Cara doesn't seem to be doing too well. She's hot and was tossing and turning a lot. I went to look for Craig, but he's not in his place. Did you see him out there?"

"No, maybe he went a different direction," Magpie said, her voice strong and sure.

"Yeah, alright. We need to let him know in the morning that Cara needs to go home," Donita replied and rolled over to go back to sleep.

Brandi and Magpie glanced at each other, a message passing between them. No matter what, this would go to their graves with them. Magpie smiled and closed her eyes. She was good at keeping secrets.

The next morning, she was up before the rest of them and went out to start a fire. She considered what they should do now. Craig had led the way to the checkpoint, so the rest of them weren't aware of the way back or forward outside of the overgrown trail they'd been following, which sometimes he veered off of. He had to have some sort of map in his stuff, and his compass. The radio. They could call for help. Magpie got up and walked toward his structure when something stopped her in her tracks.

Not something, someone.

Craig.

He wandered out of the woods toward his sleeping spot, freezing Magpie in place. Half his face was crushed in, and his arm was twisted backward, yet he didn't seem to notice. Jack and Danny woke up and went to the wood line to relieve themselves. When they came back, they saw Magpie staring at Craig's structure and stopped.

"What are you doing?" Jack asked.

Magpie turned toward him, then to Craig. Danny walked right past him, peering into the structure, and shrugged. He turned back to Magpie. "Where's Craig?"

Craig was literally within arm's reach, but Danny didn't see him. Magpie let out a breath of relief. He didn't see him because only she could. Because Craig was dead. She tried to block out the mutilated man as she answered. "Don't know, He wasn't there when I got up to start the fire. Maybe he went to gather wood or something."

Jack stoked the fire and grinned. "Maybe a bear got him."

Kinda.

Magpie glanced back at Craig and wondered if he knew she could see him. He seemed to be struggling with the fact that he couldn't open his pack. His hands passed right through it. He didn't know he was dead. That could be a problem. He'd follow them, thinking he was still their guide. Or worse, want to hurt Brandi. Finish what he started.

Luckily, she knew how to fix that. She needed the other kids to go elsewhere, so she thought of a way to make that happen. "Hey, can you two check the woods for him? Maybe grab some wood while you're out there."

Danny didn't look convinced, listening to a younger girl, but Jack nudged him. "Maybe we can find some bear shit."

Danny laughed and the two went off in search of Craig, wood, and bear shit. Magpie knew the others would be stirring soon, so she needed to move fast. She sat down cross-legged in front of the fire and closed her eyes. She settled her mind and unlatched the door. When she opened her eyes, a young man in his late teens or early twenties in worn overalls was sitting in front of her, his dirty-blond hair falling over his gray eyes. He watched her, and she could feel a sadness coming off him.

"I'm Magpie and I need your help. What's your name?"

"Tyler."

"Tyler, see that man over there? He died, but doesn't know it yet. I need you to escort him over."

Tyler's eyes flitted over to where Craig was trying to understand why he couldn't touch anything, then back at Magpie. "Who is he?"

"He was our guide, but he fell and died," Magpie explained, omitting the other details.

Tyler stared at Craig, then shook his head. "He's between two fires. I can remove him temporarily, but he will still be connected to here. Something is keeping him tied to this plane."

Magpie knew the term. Between two fires meant he was caught. Unable to move forward or back. Which meant he had done something in this life or another that prevented him from being allowed to transition. That could be a problem.

Souls like that clung to whatever was familiar from their living time. They tried to get back to what they knew, not totally understanding their fate.

"Can you remove him from here for now? I don't want him hanging around or following us," she inquired, hoping Tyler could lead Craig away, so they could leave him behind.

Tyler considered for a moment, then stood up. "I can't promise he won't show back up. At least, until he stood for what he did."

"What did he do?"

"I can't say, I'm not privy to that. Only that he can't move forward until he's held accountable for it on your side. I can take him with me, but he will be in a state of suspension."

Magpie understood. Knowing Craig was willing to rape and kill Brandi, she suspected it wasn't the first time he'd tried to harm someone. Or *did* harm someone. She watched their former guide fumble through his new reality.

She sighed. "Okay, do that. You said he might be able to come back?" she asked.

"If he realizes he's dead while he's in suspension, he may be able to come back because this will be a stronger draw. Did he hurt you?" Tyler answered.

"Not me, but another girl with us. She's still asleep," Magpie explained.

"I see. So, if he comes to grips with his demise, he may latch on to any of the last people who saw him alive. I can't stop that from happening."

Junior, Brandi, or Magpie. Magpie had to make sure if Craig came back, he came to her, so she could handle it. "Is there any way to prevent him from latching onto someone? Like a talisman, or something?"

Tyler nodded. "Blood. Spirits will be drawn by a bloody talisman. You must cover a stone with it."

"Whose?"

"The blood of the one who last touched him would be the

strongest," Tyler explained.

Junior. Magpie would figure that out later. Right now, she needed to make sure she protected everyone else. "On a stone? What if that person is bleeding? Will he latch onto them or the bloody stone?"

"The stone. The talisman is stronger than the person since their spirit is constantly in a state of chaos, but the stone is not. Spirits like inanimate objects because they are more stable than the living."

Magpie nodded. "I understand. Will you take him with you for now?"

Tyler smiled. "I will. It's been nice talking to you, Magpie."

Spirits, or ghosts, often told her this. While they had an existence on the other side, they often liked to visit the living. "It's been nice talking to you, too, Tyler. Thank you."

He got up and moved over to Craig, who was now sitting, confused, staring at his hands. Tyler reached down and touched Craig on the shoulder. The guide jerked and stared up at Tyler. He shook his head slowly, not understanding what was happening to him. Tyler crouched down and wrapped his arms around Craig, who was too stunned to protest. A blue vibration encased both of them, and in a moment, they faded from view.

Jack and Danny came out of the trees carrying wood and dropped the piles next to the fire. Jack tipped his head at Magpie, who was still sitting with her legs crossed by the fire, her eyes partially closed. "What are you doing, Magpie? Meditation?"

Magpie opened her eyes fully, letting the connection to the spirit world sever. "Something like that. You see Craig out there?"

Danny shook his head. "Nope. No bear shit, either."

"Sorry?" Magpie replied, trying not to laugh. Danny looked truly disappointed.

The rest of the teens began to stir, and Brandi came out, her face concerned. "We really need to get help for Cara, like yesterday. She's totally out of it and is burning up."

Magpie got up and pointed to Craig's structure. "Craig has a radio, we can try to call out on that. He must've gone for a hike or something. He's not here."

The two girls went to his empty structure and began digging through his pack. There was no map, but they found the radio. Magpie tried rotating the knobs, but it wouldn't turn on. She shook it and flipped it over. Nothing was happening, no matter what she did. She pried off the battery case and saw it was empty. No batteries. But he'd been calling out on it. Or appeared like he was. She sifted through his pack looking for batteries, discovering there were none. The radio didn't work and probably never had. He'd been faking the calls all along.

That's when she heard Brandi gasp and glanced over. Brandi was holding another bag open. Magpie peered into it. Inside was rope, duct tape, and a knife. However, that wasn't all. There was something else in the pack that made both girls shudder in fear and realize Craig was never there as their guide. He had his own talisman of sorts. One that made their blood run cold and realize how close they'd come to harm.

A woman's bra, saturated and crusted in dried blood.

CHAPTER 5

P erhaps, Craig had been a guide for Wilderness Reset at some point since he knew the trails and checkpoints well, but considering what they found in the bag and his behavior about the other guide, the girls knew that being their guide wasn't his plan this time around. This time, he had his own intentions.

Magpie thought about how they were notified to meet at that spot to take the hike. It matched what had been laid out in the information Wilderness Reset had provided to them initially. They would meet at a drop-off point and be greeted by two guides to be taken through the forest on hikes that led to checkpoints. So it wasn't totally off-kilter. The strange parts were that the other guide didn't show up, Craig wasn't actually communicating with anyone from Wilderness Reset, and he was acting strange. He'd set off internal alarms in her from the beginning.

After they found the pack, Brandi said she wanted to

tell Junior about it. Magpie felt that was safe enough since he knew Craig's intent with Brandi. They needed to figure out a plan now, anyhow, and Junior was technically the oldest, about to turn sixteen in a couple of weeks. Brandi went to get him, and Magpie took the moment to read her spirit messages. She closed her eyes and tuned in, hearing fragmented words accompanied by flashing images. She understood what they were telling her and opened her eyes just as Brandi and Junior came back.

Junior crouched in the structure, staring at the bloody bra. He shook his head. "What the hell is that?"

"I think maybe it belonged to the other guide, the one who didn't show up. She was a woman, and it seemed weird the way he was acting about her. He would've killed me if you two hadn't found us," Brandi expressed, her words shaky.

Junior took Brandi's hand and sat down beside her. "We did, and now he's gone. Hopefully."

"He is. Look, Cara is in bad shape. Craig was doing something strange with us, but I believe Wilderness Reset will know something is wrong and send people to find us. I think you two should stay here with Cara in case they come to the checkpoints to track us," Magpie said.

Brandi frowned. "Shouldn't we all stay here?"

Magpie shook her head. "I don't think so. We need food. I think we should split up, and the rest of us should go on ahead to see if we can find help that way. At least, get to the next checkpoint to gather the food. I sort of know the area, and there are homes scattered back in these woods. This way, we are putting out a call for help in two ways. I found a stash of food in Craig's stuff. Mostly granola bars and dried fruit, but it should help you until someone comes."

Junior looked unsure and glanced around. "Did he have anything else?"

Brandi and Magpie glanced at each other for a moment. Brandi cleared her throat. "A knife, rope, and duct tape."

His eyes grew wide as he put his hand to his mouth with the realization of the danger they'd been in. "Damn."

"Oh, and a gun," Magpie added. "We don't have much time, though, so we need to come up with a plan. Like I said, I think you two should stay with Cara. Keep the fire going to let rescuers know where you are. If they come before we get back, let them know the rest of us went north to find help. We'll stick to the trail, which should take us to the next checkpoint."

"Are you sure?" Brandi asked, concerned.

Magpie shook her head. "No, but what choice do we have? There isn't enough food here for all of us, and the next checkpoint should have another supply of food waiting. If nothing else, we can get that and come back with it. On the way, I'll try and find a house to call for help. Plus, those who have cell phones will keep checking for service."

It was a rough plan, but the only one they had. Magpie was correct in that they didn't have enough food for the whole group. At a minimum, someone needed to go to the next checkpoint. Leaving only the two of them with Cara would ensure the little food they did have there wouldn't run out. Their families were told to check in every couple of days with Wilderness Reset for updates, so that would set off alarms with the company when parents called in to check up on teens who weren't even supposed to be out there.

"What about the gun?" Junior asked.

Magpie tipped her head, considering who it would help most. "Can you shoot?"

Junior dropped his head. "No."

"I can," said Brandi, chewing her painted thumbnail.

This surprised them both, but Magpie nodded. "Okay, so you two keep it with you for protection."

"What about you?" Junior asked. "You're the ones going out into the forest alone. That's dangerous. Can you shoot?"

"I can, but with Cara being unable to move, you need to

be able to protect the camp from animals. We will be on the go, so we can run and hide if needed. It makes more sense for you to keep it on you."

It was all a risk, however, Magpie knew if they didn't move fast, Cara might not make it. She could read a toxicity in the sick girl, and they had no medicine for it. All they found in Craig's stuff and the left behind supplies were pain and fever pills, bandages, and peroxide for first aid supplies. Nothing that would help Cara heal.

"Okay," Brandi said. "Should we tell the others? What do we say about Craig?"

They couldn't tell the truth, but they could tell a partial truth. Magpie leaned forward. "We'll tell them he never came back last night, so Junior went to look for him and saw his body at the bottom of a cliff. He tried to get down to him, but there was no safe way to traverse the cliff. The rest can be true. No radio, splitting up, that kind of stuff."

They agreed and called a meeting around the fire. Everyone seemed confused and kept glancing back at Craig's structure as if they expected him to emerge from it. Junior waited until everyone except Cara settled around the fire and called the meeting to order with a raise of his hand.

"Hey, everyone, I know there has been some confusion as to where Craig is. I have some bad news, I'm afraid. I went to look for him after a bit and saw his body down a cliff at the bottom. I guess he went to relieve himself in the night and fell in the dark. He's dead."

"How do you know he's dead? Can we go see?" Danny asked, a little too excited about the possibility.

"No. It's not safe. I couldn't get to him, but trust me, he's dead," Junior answered.

"What do we do now?" Donita asked, her eyes filled with worry.

"Brandi and I are going to stay back with Cara, who is very sick, while the rest of you go on to the next checkpoint to gather the supplies. We are hoping Wilderness Reset sends someone this way soon. The radio Craig had on him isn't working, so we can't call for help."

"Why would they do that?" inquired Jack.

They couldn't tell the rest of the kids what they'd found or the conclusion they'd come to about Craig's intent. Magpie jumped in. "They need to restock the food for the next group, right? They'd have to send someone up to do that, eventually."

"When does the next group come through, though?" Chase asked.

"I don't know, but considering the trail is pretty worn in areas, they must come on a regular basis. Maybe weekly?" Junior answered.

"So, if Junior, Cara, and Brandi are staying and the rest of us are going on ahead, who will be our guide?" Jack questioned.

"Me," Magpie replied.

"Why you?" Danny asked, almost indignantly.

"Because Magpie knows the area. She grew up here and was taught how to survive," Brandi interjected, surprising Magpie. She didn't know Brandi was aware of her skills.

"That's true. My family lives off the land, and we are familiar with these woods."

"Didn't you, like, kill your grandfather? How can we trust you?" Danny pushed back.

"Stabbed him, yeah. I'm not asking you to trust me, Danny. I'm saying we need to go to the next checkpoint for food. There isn't enough here for more than Junior, Brandi, and Cara. Even that is a stretch."

"Why is it Brandi and Junior staying here? Why not send them on and others stay?" Donita questioned.

It was a valid point. They'd only made that choice amongst themselves, and it needed to be a group decision. Murmurs ran through the group, and Chase raised his hand.

"I want to go with Magpie to the next checkpoint."

"Me too," said Jack, surprising Magpie. Danny agreed, wanting to go wherever Jack went. That left Donita.

She glanced around and sighed. "Alright, I can't leave you alone with all these boys. I'll go, as well, to balance things out."

That settled it. They went over other details and timelines. They'd head out after breakfast to make the most use of daylight and make it to the checkpoint by nightfall. They'd sleep there and then head back with food the next morning. Hopefully, they'd either find a house along the way or someone would come to where Junior, Brandi, and Cara were by then.

As they were getting up to get ready, Danny spoke up. "You know, in horror movies, they all die in the end because they split up."

If he meant it as a joke, none of them took it that way. Junior glanced at Brandi, who looked at Magpie. Were they doing the wrong thing?

Magpie shrugged. "This isn't a movie, is it? What choice do we have?"

Danny laughed. "I was just kidding, Magpie. Geez. Lighten up."

Magpie reconsidered leading this bunch into the woods. Danny and Jack thought everything was a joke, and Donita seemed doubtful about going. Chase, at least, was on board. She looked at him, and he put his hand in the air as if to say, "Ignore him", in reference to Danny.

Before they left, Magpie pulled Junior aside, holding a stone in her hand. He tipped his head, confused as he stared at the rock. "What's that?"

"I need you to put this on the far side of the campsite," she explained. "But one more thing. You need to bleed on it."

He laughed for a second, then got serious. "This some kind of witchcraft thing?"

Magpie tipped her head, measuring her words. "Not exactly, but it should protect you three."

"From what?"

44

From Craig.

She couldn't say that, though. She didn't want to scare him. "Just trust me, alright? It's a talisman."

Junior eyed her, then nodded. "Okay, here, give it to me."

He took out a pocket knife and drew the blade across his thumb, wincing in pain. Blood welled up, and he smeared it across the top of the rock. He walked over and set it on the edge of the campsite, glancing back at her with a mix of humor and acceptance. Regardless of her reasoning, he understood she was trying to keep them safe.

Magpie hoped it would be enough to keep the errant spirit at bay.

CHAPTER 6

T he group going on ahead gathered their packs and head-
    ed out before noon to make time in the daylight. Magpie
followed the thin, worn trail, which she hoped led to the next
checkpoint. It was the only clear path leading from the site, so
it had to be the one.

They hiked in silence for much of the day, outside of
Jack and Danny cutting up, feeling like a much smaller group.
Chase fell in with Donita, sensing Magpie wanted to be alone
at the front. She did, but not because she didn't want Chase
around. She genuinely liked his company but was lost in her
own thoughts as she tracked through the forest, considering
how they would get back to civilization.

Magpie had taken the knife and rope from Craig's pack,
figuring any extra supplies could help. She shifted her pack,
feeling the weight of his ill-intended gear against her back.
With only the knife as protection, they were taking a huge
risk. Magpie also had something extra, though. Something

the rest of them couldn't see or comprehend. It gave her great comfort, knowing she wasn't only relying on her skills to get them home. She turned and smiled at her unseen companion, who'd fallen in step with her. He smiled back with a tip of his head.

Tyler had joined them.

Magpie was glad for it, feeling the gravity of their situation. Craig was dead, the radio was a bust, they had no map, and were split into two groups. Even Jack and Danny, who spent most of their time together cracking jokes and messing around, fell into a strange bubble of quietness as the day wore on. Chase and Donita talked softly as they hiked. Magpie communicated with Tyler using her mind, and he told her about his history.

He was born in nineteen forty-nine and was raised in the area. His father was a farmer, and his mother died in childbirth, taking his newborn baby brother with him. His father was a hard man, taking his frustrations out on his only surviving family member, Tyler. Tyler ran away and joined the military, losing his life in the Vietnam War. Magpie asked why he wasn't wearing a uniform, as many of the ghosts she met wore what they died in. He told her it was because he missed home and wanted nothing more than to go back. However, after his death, his father committed suicide. The bank took the farm, leveling the old, decrepit farmhouse to the ground. A subdivision went up in its place. There was no home left to go back to.

This made Magpie sad, though she'd become accustomed to hearing the depressing stories of ghosts she communicated with. In a way, they were still trapped, still bound to their living time. Some because of an unresolved issue, others because they weren't ready to move on yet from this world. Tyler was part of that group. His grief of leaving home and his father kept him from letting go and transitioning on. She liked his company but was determined to help him work through it and release him from this plane.

By lunchtime, the group was ready to rest for a bit and ate the last bit of food they had. Hopefully, they'd find food at the next checkpoint. If not, they were in serious trouble. Chase came over and sat next to Magpie.

"Is it okay if I hang out with you?" he asked, even though he was already sitting near her.

She smiled. "Of course. I saw you chatting with Donita earlier. She's nice."

"She is. Figured we needed to get to know one another better since we are on an unspecified journey."

Magpie laughed at his description. That was one way to put it. She handed Chase half her sandwich. She was still struggling with eating the provided food, and he seemed to be eyeing it. He grinned and took it without question, scarfing it down in a couple of bites. They sat in silence, gazing around the lush, dense forest. They had yet to come across a house. Magpie supposed Wilderness Reset made their trails away from towns and homes, so the kids didn't try to escape or harass residents.

After they finished eating, the group gathered their belongings and headed on up the trail. This time, Chase walked with Magpie, and she noticed Tyler had disappeared. She hoped he'd come back at some point. His company made her feel safer, more at ease; she wasn't sure why. Chase chatted about his life back home, his brother, and school. Magpie found it comforting. She didn't go to public school. Her family homeschooled the children, even her coming on this trip was out of their wheelhouse. They didn't trust outsiders and had a way of dealing with issues within the fold.

As night fell, they hadn't yet come upon the checkpoint, and Magpie feared she'd gotten them lost. She kept moving along the trail, deciding when to call it and have them huddle down for the night. Around the time she was ready to give up, she made out three pointed roofs and saw the checkpoint up ahead. Invigorated by the site, the group ran the rest of the way, heading straight for the structures. As before, there was packaged food, firewood, and water left for them.

Too tired to start a fire, they ate food straight out of the cans and bedded down. Magpie set aside the extra food rationed for Junior, Brandi, and Cara and placed it in her backpack. It was heavy, but they could head back in the morning, which at least was mostly downhill. She let her eyes close and slipped into a dreamless sleep.

The sound of screams woke her in the early morning hours, and she peered out to see a large black bear blocking the boys' structure. It had obviously smelled the food they ate and came to help itself. Jack and Danny were pressed against the back of the structure as Chase was fending off the bear with a walking stick. The bear, however, was more determined than that and kept swiping at Chase, its mouth opened in a growl.

Magpie saw Tyler appear, and he motioned to the empty structure meant for the guides. He was letting Magpie know there was something in there that could help. She eyed the bear and darted for the structure, distracting the bear with her presence for the moment. It roared at her, making her blood run cold. She dove in, praying the bear wouldn't follow her. In the pack left there, Magpie found a flare gun and yanked it out, shoving the cartridge in. She'd never used a flare gun before, but figured it couldn't be much different than an actual gun.

Aiming toward the bear, Magpie closed one eye and fired, sending the flare haphazardly through the campsite. This startled the hungry bear, who reared up and stumbled back, confused. However, it didn't run away as she hoped it would. It retreated to the outskirts of the campsite and hovered there, still wanting their food but scared enough to stay back.

Chase peered out and gazed over to where Magpie was crouched with the flare gun. Donita was in the opening of the other structure, waiting to see what to do. Everyone was looking to Magpie for guidance she didn't have. She saw there were two more flares in the bag and considered firing another one, but thought they might need them to get rescued. The bear didn't move, unsure.

Chase ran for the structure Magpie was in, diving past her once he got there. Donita did the same, and they huddled together, their bodies shaking with fear. Danny and Jack hadn't emerged, so Magpie suspected they were frozen in terror. It was a three-way stand-off. The bear, the food, and the teens. They couldn't afford to give the bear the little bit of food they had, and it was not leaving without it.

She turned to Chase and Donita. "We need to get to Jack and Danny. Do you have your packs with you?"

Donita bobbed her head, pointing to her pack she'd dropped by the opening. "I have my backpack, but not my sleeping bag."

"Mine's in with Jack and Danny," Chase whispered.

"Okay, we need to make a run for it. Get to them and see if we can scare the bear off," Magpie said.

"Can't they come to us?" Donita asked.

Magpie shrugged. "Do you honestly think they will?"

"No, I guess not."

"On the count of three, grab these supply bags and get ready to run. I have the flare gun if we need it," Magpie instructed. "Are you ready?"

They both looked unsure but nodded, clutching the sacks from the structure and Donita's pack. Magpie took a deep breath, wondering if they could outrun a bear. They were about to find out one way or another. "One, two, three, go!"

They got up and hustled as fast as they could to the other structure. The bear spied them and charged in their direction. There was no way they'd make it there before the bear got to them. Chase tripped and fell, landing face-first on the ground. Magpie turned and grabbed his arm, attempting to get him to his feet. Donita had made it to the structure, however, the bear blocked their way, turning and growling at Chase and Magpie.

They were done for. Chase got to his feet, but the bear came at them, ready to attack. Chase closed his eyes, waiting for the pain. Magpie froze, trying to aim the flare gun, when a familiar figure stepped between them and the bear. Tyler waved his arms, jumping up and down. The bear halted, confused by the figure in front of it that appeared out of nowhere. It stepped back with one paw in the air, trying to comprehend its new situation. It sniffed and made what could only be explained as a whimper. It backed away and wandered into the woods, pausing to glance back before moving on.

Magpie and Chase ran for the structure, scrambling in before the bear changed its mind and returned. Chase grabbed his stuff, throwing it over his shoulder. Magpie peered at Jack and Danny, motioning to their packs. "Let's go before it comes back."

The boys glanced at each other, too afraid to move when Donita raised her voice. "Now!"

That got them moving, and they stumbled out of the structure as Donita went to grab her sleeping bag. Magpie gathered her belongings and let out a heavy breath. With the food and flare gun, Magpie felt better about their chances. They headed back down the trail to where Brandi, Cara, and Junior were waiting. Shaken and exhausted, no one had the energy to do more than trudge along, so it was a quiet hike. Magpie estimated if they moved at the current pace, they'd make it back to the previous checkpoint before dusk as long as they didn't stop to eat.

Chase might not be too thrilled about that prospect.

Tyler had disappeared again as quickly as he came, and Magpie silently thanked him for his help. She hoped he'd rejoin them at some point. Hearing a rustling in the woods behind them, she paused and gazed back. Nothing was in sight, and she knew plenty of animals lived and made sounds in the forest. It sounded large, but deer often wandered the woods.

The second time she heard it, though, the hair on her arms rose, and she put her hand up to stop the group. She put her finger to her lips to let them know to be quiet as she scanned around the area. They slowed and peered around. The forest fell silent, but Magpie knew better. Something was out there watching them.

They were being stalked.

Chapter 7

J ust as Magpie was about to warn the others, a large black
shape came barreling at them, crushing brush around it
in its wake. The bear! It was back and it was angry. The
teens scattered, running in every direction. Magpie tried to
get them to stay together, but no one was listening in their
fright. Jack and Danny ran in one direction, Chase in another,
Magpie and Donita in yet a different one. The bear stopped,
not sure which group to go after, then decided on the sole
runner.

Chase.

Magpie halted and loaded the flare gun with shaking
hands, taking aim at the determined bear. She steadied her
breathing and aimed the flare gun. The trigger had a little
resistance, and she pulled back hard, praying it would hit the
mark. The flare shot out and made a beeline for the bear's rear
end. It struck the bear dead on, sending the creature roaring
through the trees in confusion and pain.

If it hadn't been scared away last time, it certainly had now with the direct hit. The girls ran up to Chase, who was crouched and trembling, his life having flashed before his eyes. He stood and wrapped his arms around Magpie in gratitude. She could smell the terror in his sweat and hugged him back. Donita joined them, and they stood until their hearts settled. Jack and Danny were still nowhere to be seen.

They moved throughout the woods calling for the boys, when they found them huddled behind a tree trunk. The group sat together and tried to calm themselves. Once everyone had released their fear and were ready to move on, Magpie scanned around them. Nothing looked familiar, and her heart fell. They were in serious trouble now.

The trail they'd been following was completely gone, absorbed by the forest they'd run through to get away from the beast. They were totally lost.

Panic came over Magpie as she realized they were deep in the forest without a clue about which way to go. She didn't want to alarm the others, so she got up and scoped out the area for some sign of a trail or humanity. Oddly, she came across a row of small rocks lined up about a foot apart, leading in a certain direction. Or maybe they were meant to lead wherever they were already. Either way, her logic was that someone had to have placed them there for some reason. It was their only chance to get back on track.

"Hey, come here!" she yelled to the other kids, who were still recovering from their encounter with the bear. Chase, especially, after being singled out by the angry animal.

"Why?" Jack asked, pushing back against her perceived authority.

"I found something strange over here. Come look," Magpie replied more as an order than a request. She understood they were all shaken up, but they had a limited amount of daylight and didn't want to be stuck in the forest overnight.

Danny groaned and got up, stomping over to where Magpie was. The others followed behind like they might drop at any moment, shoulders slumped and feet like lead. Once they all gathered, Magpie pointed at the rock line, which seemed to stretch through the brush until it disappeared out of view.

"There. Those rocks must have been placed by a human as they are way too symmetrical to have simply ended up that way on their own. Or not likely to have been moved by an animal," she explained.

"Or Bigfoot," Jack joked.

Considering their last encounter with the bear, no one found it funny. Chase glanced around them, almost as if he was expecting to see a creature emerge from behind a tree. They instinctively drew closer to one another and stared at the rocks. Donita shrugged and began walking beside the line. Magpie waited for the others to trail behind and brought up the rear, letting Donita lead the way for a bit. As long as they had markers, they had something to follow.

After about an hour, Donita fell back as Magpie took over. The rocks continued, which was bizarre. They'd ended or begun, depending on their purpose, exactly where the teens found themselves lost, but now stretched on forever it seemed. Each almost the exact the same distance apart from the others. Like a curious linear symbol. Magpie felt the hair raise on her arms and began to question her decision for them to follow the peculiar stone trail.

What if it was a trap?

She mentally laughed at herself. A trap set by whom? For what purpose? How would they know the kids would end up at that exact spot in the woods? Sure, it was strange, but she couldn't read into it more than that. A weird coincidence was all. A thought dawned on her, and she tried to shake it off. What if the trail had been placed by another lost hiker and they made it as far as where the kids found it, then died? A shudder ran through her, and she took a deep breath. No sense in making up crazy theories. There hadn't been a body or bones to discover.

As she was thinking that, the stones ran out. Simply ended in the middle of the woods as abruptly as they'd begun. Started and stopped with no rhyme or reason. Magpie paused and peered around, hoping to see something telling her which way to go. Chase practically ran into her back as he'd been looking down as he was hiking.

"Oh, sorry, Magpie. Why are we stopped?" he asked, peering around for clarity.

Magpie pointed to the ground, and he saw the last stone in the line. The others came up and gathered around, their faces twisted in confusion. Danny raised his hand in the air in question. "Now what do we do?"

"I don't know. Let me think," Magpie mumbled, more to herself than anyone else. They were once again without direction, lost in the woods. It was easy to get scared, however, they needed to consider their options.

"What's there to think about?" Jack shouted as he waved his hands near his head. "Fuck! Can't you just shoot off the flare gun to try and let someone know we're here?"

Seeing the group was getting agitated, Magpie knew she needed to move fast before it erupted into chaos. If she shot off the flare gun, they'd have to remain where they were in the off chance someone saw it. That would put them at risk as they had no shelter and were exposed to animals and the elements.

She shook her head. "No, not here. Wherever we shoot it off, we need to be able to stay and wait for rescue. Do you want to stay right here in this spot?"

Jack didn't answer and stormed away a few yards. He stood with his arms crossed, staring at her sullenly. He wasn't disagreeing with her, but he wasn't making an effort to agree, either. It was hard to connect to the spirits when it wasn't calm, but Magpie tried, anyway, closing her eyes.

"What are you doing?" Danny inquired with a mixture of irritation and humor.

She put her finger in the air to let him know to give her a moment. "Shhh."

"Did she seriously just shush me?" Danny asked the others, irritated.

Chase jumped in. "Chill out, dude. She's trying to help. Give her a minute to get her bearings. Unless you have a better idea of what to do now."

Danny didn't and joined Jack away from the group.

When Magpie opened her eyes, she gazed around. At first, she didn't see anything out of the ordinary. Then, on the edge of the woods, she saw Tyler and knew they needed to follow him. Ghosts couldn't lead the living, but they could go in a way they were drawn. So Magpie couldn't ask him to be their guide, but she could ask him to show her a place he was familiar with. If he was there, he was from the area. He might be able to guide them to some sort of human-made place. It was their only chance.

"This way," she insisted to the others.

"Are you sure?" Donita asked, her dark brows knitted together.

Magpie nodded. Tyler was still heading south, she thought, so in the general direction of the previous checkpoint. They weren't getting off track that much as long as they continued in that direction. "Yeah. We need to keep going south."

"That's south?" Danny asked. "Do you have a compass or something?"

She didn't. That had likely gone over the ledge with Craig. She pointed to the sun, making it up as she went along. She actually had no clue if that was right, but she couldn't really tell them she was following a ghost. She shrugged and began walking without answering. The less she said, the less likely she was to say something completely off. The others fell in behind her as they moved slowly through the tangled brush. Tyler let Magpie catch up to him, and they conversed silently as they hiked.

"Are you taking me to where you grew up around here?" Magpie asked.

"No. There's nothing left of my home, so I don't go back. There are homes there, but it is much farther than you know. We couldn't make it by nightfall."

"I'm sorry. Where are we going, then?"

Tyler frowned, seeming to not want to answer. "The only place I know around here we can get to before dark. A storm is coming, so it will give you shelter. But you can't stay there long, or you won't get out."

"Why? What is it?"

He grimaced. "When I was a boy, they opened this place out in the middle of nowhere for people whose families wanted them away from them. Or those the state decided were irredeemable."

"Irredeemable? In what way? Like criminals?"

"No, not criminals, but they were treated that way. People with mental and physical disabilities that made them unable to function in society, according to doctors and politicians," Tyler explained.

"Oh. That's terrible. So, like an asylum?" Magpie asked.

"An institution, I suppose. I used to ride my bike over there when I was around ten or eleven and watch from the woods. It was strange, being set out in the woods with only a thin dirt road leading to it. People called it the 'loony bin'. At first, it was quiet and seemed like they were taking care of the patients in there. However, as years went on, I heard more screams and crying coming from the place. It scared me, so I quit going," Tyler answered.

"Is it still open?"

"No, it was shut down decades ago when a woman tried to set it on fire. The authorities came and found people chained to beds, sinks, and pipes. Some were already dead. A few survived, but all have died since. Sometimes, their ghosts come back and wander the grounds like they forgot something there. They never go inside. The place doesn't exist anymore to humans. It's not on any map."

Magpie stopped and stared at Tyler, trying to understand what he meant by that. "But it's still there, that's where you are taking us."

Tyler nodded and met her eyes. "It's still there, yes. If you know what to look for."

"I see, and you know what to look for?"

"I do."

"Why can't other humans find it if it was built by them?" Magpie knew they were treading into tenuous territory.

There were places that appeared and disappeared at times. Then, there were people who wandered in and never came out. Sometimes, those places simply were, like any other human-made place. The structure itself wasn't what shifted. Other times, it was the building that shifted, as well. Ultimately, it was the ancient soil the structure was built on that carried the transition between the human world and the spirit world. Knowing this, Magpie suspected what Tyler was about to say before he said it.

Tyler paused and peered through the trees, seeing things the others couldn't see with the naked eye. He tugged at his overalls' strap and met her eyes with lifetimes of heaviness.

"The land is tainted."

CHAPTER 8

"Why don't some of the ghosts go inside? You said they come to the building and wander around outside, can they not go in?" Magpie asked, her brows knitted. Something about what he was telling her was sending off alarms in her soul.

"I don't know for sure. They didn't die in there, I know that. The ones that died inside those walls, I never see outside. I'm sure some transitioned, but not all. The ones that died elsewhere don't ever want to step inside. I can't either, not that I would want to if I could."

Magpie considered that. The ghosts she talked to were almost always outside. The few she saw inside had been former residents of the home who must've passed away there or wanted to go back. She'd never considered their restrictions between their reality and the human world. "Can ghosts not go where they haven't been inside in life before?"

"Not places with a roof. I can move anywhere except

inside man-made structures I wasn't in when I was alive. I died outside, so I can only be outside or in a structure I was in before in life. Churches, stores, homes, schools, things like that. My home is gone. Sometimes I visit my high school. It's not the same, though. Everything has changed. Moved on without me," Tyler replied, his voice sounding faded for a moment.

"Why are you still here? I mean, tied to this plane? Can't you go on?" Magpie asked.

A ghost who hadn't transitioned was usually trapped by a belief or unfinished business. Sometimes, they didn't know they'd died, but Tyler obviously did. So, something else was holding him back.

"I'm not sure. I simply am."

Magpie felt bad for Tyler. Away from home, away from family, wandering the forest for decades all alone. She thought about where he was taking them. "The institution? It didn't burn down, then?"

"No, the fire department got the fire out before it did too much damage."

"How'd they get out here so fast, considering the location being so far from any town?" Magpie wondered mentally to Tyler. They were nowhere near civilization, and the terrain was less than vehicle-friendly.

"I can't say, but I do know there were other forces involved, outside of humans. They knew what Margaret was up to, I think, long before she went to start that fire," Tyler answered.

"Like ghosts?"

"No, ghosts are transient, temporary. They don't want to cause harm. These are ancient forces. Not good ones, either. Haints. This land is tainted. Has always been since the dawn of time."

Magpie knew those all too well, the ancient forces he was speaking about. Dark spirits. They'd gotten hold of her grandpa. The problem with being tuned into the spirit world was it allowed anything to pass through if they weren't careful. Not only was her grandpa not careful, he welcomed them in, believing they would give him otherworldly powers. The ability to rule over man like a god. Instead, they manipulated him and turned him into a hateful, abusive person. Then, they convinced him that Magpie needed to be sacrificed for him to fully complete the process.

To earn his place in their world.

She was warned by her guides and knew what was coming that night when he lured her away. She was ready, a knife hidden in her skirt folds. She wasn't trying to kill him, she was trying to release the demon inside him, holding him captive and trying to take her with them. He was still her grandpa. The man who bounced her on his knee when she was small and called her his little bird. He'd always been opportunistic and angry, a bigoted country man who didn't like anyone outside of his own family. He'd been loving and protective with his grandchildren, though. However, once the spirits took hold of him, he was more than willing to destroy everything in his path to gain power.

Including his own kin.

"Who was the woman who set the fire? Was she one of the patients?" Magpie asked Tyler as she stepped carefully over a rotting log.

Tyler shook his head. "No, she was a local woman. She spoke to spirits, aligned ones. They reached out to her because she'd been through her own suffering and would listen to them. They told her to go out to help the people trapped in there. When she got to the institution, she saw the horrible torture the patients were going through and tried to stop it. No one believed her, and the surviving patients asked her to put them out of their misery. She attempted freeing them first, but couldn't break the chains trapping them to their beds. Deciding to end it all, she went down to the basement to start the fire. The only way to drive the dark spirits away was to remove everything and close the door in-between worlds. However, they fought her off. She wasn't able to complete the task."

"Oh. So, are we safe to go in there?"

"It's been empty for decades. Even if there is activity in there, you should be fine for the night. Don't stay any longer, though, and stay near the door out, no matter what. The haints have a way of tricking people into getting lost."

The haints. Magpie was very familiar with the ill-intentioned spirits. Haints fed off fear and used their wiles to harm humans. It fed their energy and made them stronger. She didn't want to cross them, so she took Tyler's warning seriously. Hopefully, the place had been abandoned for so long, the dark spirits had moved on in search of fresh prey and higher activity elsewhere. Even so, the threat wasn't to be taken lightly.

The teens only had a little food left, so either way, they couldn't stay for too long. Long enough to set off the flare and hopefully be rescued. Maybe find the old road to the institution, which had to lead somewhere, eventually, if rescue didn't come in time.

Magpie turned to Tyler, realizing how young he was when he died. Barely even a man. "What was her name? The woman who tried to burn the place down?"

Tyler met her eyes, knowing something she didn't, then nodded, measuring his words. "Her name was Margaret Blankenship."

Margaret Blankenship. The name triggered a spark deep in Magpie's head. A distant connection tied to photos and stories. Seeing her past chubby child hands patting a black and white photo as her mother scooped her up in her lap to tell her a tale. A story of a brave woman who stood up to outsiders and took down the dark spirits.

Magpie's family had many of these stories, but this one

in particular helped form her own passion for fighting back against the bad side. It developed a warrior part of her that knew it was on her shoulders to be the wall between that side and what was right. As a child, she saw her family split by the forces. Those who embraced the gentle sharing of two worlds and preserved that sanctity, and those who used the power behind the ability to further their own selfish agenda.

She stopped in her tracks, her mouth falling open as she put the two together. "Margaret Blankenship was my great-grandmother."

That revelation made Magpie wonder if none of this was random. If either the spirit world or the institution itself had called to her to finish Margaret's task? Or maybe it *was* random, and in time, she would've stumbled upon this place on her own and come to face the demons of the past. Somehow, she thought confronting her grandpa's evil intent might have pushed it along. As she was considering this, the hair on her arms stood up and goosebumps speckled her skin. She knew this meant she was in the presence of dark spectres, as when she called on ghosts, she never felt that way.

Ghosts felt like family.

"What the hell is that?" Chase asked, his voice unsure.

Magpie glanced at where he was staring and saw it. The crumbling structure of the former institution. It had been around thirty years since anyone was there, the walls and roof were barely standing. Bricks littered the ground where the building had given in to gravity and released its hold. Outside of the issue of it likely being haunted, Magpie wondered if it was even safe enough structurally to walk into. The group slowed their pace as if they inherently understood the danger lurking behind the walls.

Magpie stared up at the building, her instincts telling her it wasn't uninhabited as she'd hoped. Something existed within those walls. Not human. She saw Tyler watching a window on the top floor and focused in. A shape moved behind the pane of glass. It wasn't an animal, and it wasn't alive on an earthly plane. Whatever was in there had been waiting for them. Waiting for *her*. She took a deep breath to settle her nerves. She had a feeling if she went in, she'd never make it back out again.

Tyler turned and met Magpie's eyes, shaking his head in worry. "It's not safe to go in. They are still in there. They must have known you were coming. I'm sorry, I never should have brought you here."

Magpie gazed around the overgrown yard surrounding the structure and considered camping out there for the night. It seemed like the smarter decision, and she didn't want to freak the others out. Then again, there *was* the bear. It had followed them once before and may still be tracking the group. They risked attack while they were sleeping if they were out in the open.

She weighed the options when she noticed a middle-aged woman walking across the lawn out of nowhere. The woman was wearing a strange dress, almost like a housecoat and slippers, as if she'd just climbed out of bed. He hair was wild around her head, tangled and matted in spots.

Magpie went to call out to her when she realized the woman was a ghost. She was hunched slightly and walking like she was in a great deal of pain. Normally, a spirit was released from their human bonds when they died, and any struggles tied to that, however, spirits could get caught between worlds and carry their suffering with them until they were released. This woman clearly was stuck and still suffering. The woman walked around the side of the building and disappeared out of sight, either unaware of the group of teens, or she simply didn't care about their presence.

Magpie looked back at Tyler, but the spot he'd been in was empty. He was gone. Magpie assumed he didn't want to be so close to the building for fear of its power. She couldn't blame him, but she also felt they were called there for a reason.

Curiosity won over, and Magpie walked toward the massive front door. Though the structure was crumbling, the door was firmly in place, a testament to the threshold between realities.

Buildings disintegrated and fell, however, the doorways connecting worlds always remained. They were timeless and fluid. Magpie reached out and touched the large brass handle, almost being drawn by an unseen force to open it. She stroked the cool metal, feeling a vibration deep within its core.

A chill ran up her spine as she sensed they weren't alone. She turned back to face the other teens and witnessed a shocking sight. A massive army of ghosts had gathered throughout the woods behind them, filling the forest end to end. The others couldn't hear them, but they made a horrible sound which echoed from the branches. A collective howl... their faces twisted in distress with their mouths open in an ungodly scream. Magpie understood what they were trying to do, why they'd come in one united force at the very moment she touched the door.

They were warning her to stop.

CHAPTER 9

"**W**ait, are we going in there?" Donita questioned. "I don't think we should. It doesn't look safe, and it creeps me out."

Magpie shook her head, now knowing the greater danger was inside. Bear or no bear, staying outside was the smarter choice for the group. "I think we can stay outside, but if we are close to the building and shoot off the flare gun, maybe it will be easier for us to be found by rescuers. We can build a fire and hope someone sees it, or the flare. I'd rather not go inside if we can help it."

"Yeah, I'm definitely not fucking going in there," Jack retorted, throwing his bag on the ground and squatting next to it. Danny joined him as they made their line in the sand.

Magpie couldn't blame them. Outside of what she knew about the history of the institution, the place was just plain spooky. She wouldn't tell them about it being inhabited, not that they would believe her, anyway. Besides, the structure on its own was enough to make them want to stay out of it. It looked like a classic haunted house, but bigger and more daunting.

They were close enough to stop and shoot off the flare gun, so she set her backpack on the ground and dug it out. "We can camp out here. I'll fire this off and, hopefully, we'll get rescued by the morning."

After she sent the flare to the sky, the group gathered around and built a small fire. Sensing her decision, the ghosts in the forest quieted and dispersed back into the woods, disappearing out of sight as quickly as they had appeared. Tyler hadn't returned, but Magpie knew if she called on him, he'd come. The teens ate some of the food Magpie had stored for Junior, Brandi, and Cara from the last checkpoint, making sure to leave some for the morning. There was no sense in keeping it, as they were too far off track to find their way back to the others.

It was all about survival now.

Magpie really wished she had a map so she could use the institution to get her bearings as to where they might be. Though she doubted a map even would give them a clue as to where they were. She peered up at the sky, noting the location of the sun. It was getting late, and the sun was beginning to set, so she used that to get a general idea of which way to go if rescue didn't come by morning. Her family was from the area, however, not close enough for her to know exactly where she was.

Getting up to wander the grounds, Magpie set her sights on trying to find the old road. If they could find that, maybe they could follow it to civilization. A road had to lead somewhere. Donita joined her, which surprised Magpie. They hadn't really connected, and even though they were only a year apart in age, Donita seemed so much more mature and street-wise than Magpie. Even so, she appreciated the company and the chance to get to know Donita better.

They walked in silence for a few minutes when Donita turned to her. "What are you looking for?"

"Well, if there's a building, there must have been a road leading to it, right? This place has been abandoned for decades, but if we can find a way in, maybe we can find a way out."

"Oh. Wouldn't it have grown over by now?" Donita asked, taking more time to observe her surroundings.

"Probably, but mostly brush and any trees would be smaller than the others, I think. It should still have a different look. I hope, anyway. Not really sure, but figured I'd take a look while we are waiting," Magpie explained, scanning the vegetation for any differences.

"Makes sense," Donita muttered more to herself as she glanced around the area, looking for smaller trees.

They circled the building, not seeing anything that was clearly a road. Around the front of the structure, there seemed to be a section of growth that wasn't quite like the rest, but it was quickly swallowed by the forest. If there had been a road, it was long gone by now. Discouraged, they headed back to where the boys were setting up camp.

Chase saw them and waved. "Did you find anything out there?"

"No. We saw where the road might have been, but it is completely overgrown and part of the woods now. Not enough to follow," Magpie explained, defeated.

"Bummer," Chase replied as he gathered wood for the fire. "Maybe someone saw the flare and is coming to save us as we speak."

"Maybe," Magpie answered, doubting it. Something about the institution told her they built it as far away from society as possible for a reason. She also sensed things weren't quite as they seemed from the outside.

She joined Chase in gathering kindling, as Donita, Jack, and Danny cleared excess brush from the area. By the time they were all done, they had a tidy camping spot and sat down around the fire. As they'd hiked, they had gotten to know each other pretty well, but only where they were from and the trouble they'd gotten into.

Magpie decided to switch gears. "Do any of you have brothers or sisters? I have an older brother, Dante, and a younger sister, Beatrix. We call her Bea."

"Your family likes weird names, huh?" Danny teased.

Magpie shrugged. "My mother says they all mean something. She said she named me Magpie because of the old nursery rhyme."

"The nursery rhyme?" Chase asked, wrinkling his nose in confusion.

"One for sorrow, two for joy, three for a girl, four for a boy, five for silver, six for gold, seven for a secret never to be told," Magpie recited.

"What does it mean?" Donita inquired.

"I don't know exactly. She said it's about how many magpies people see at a particular time and what the number of them means. She said she knew I was a girl before I was born because things kept happening in threes, and the number seven repeated in her dreams as birds when she was pregnant with me. I guess that's why," Magpie answered, though she wasn't entirely sure herself. Her mother was often cryptic in her reasoning.

"No wonder you stabbed your grandfather," Jack joked. "Your family is strange."

Magpie ignored his jab. "So, what about your family, Jack?"

He eyed her and glanced at the ground. "Just me and my mom. My dad took off a couple of years ago. He used to visit, but as I got older, I guess he didn't like my mouth."

Magpie sensed abandonment behind his words and felt for him. Chase cleared his throat. "Opposite here. Me and my dad. My mother died when I was little. Cancer."

Donita watched him and tipped her head. "Any siblings?"

"Oh, yeah. My older brother, but he joined the army at seventeen and took off to get out of the house. He and my dad butted heads a lot. What about you, Donita?"

"Parents still together, my grandma lives with us. I have three siblings, all younger. I'm like a second mom to them."

"They must miss you," Magpie suggested.

"Ha, they're probably raiding my room as we speak. I do miss them, though," Donita replied with a sentimental twinkle in her eye.

That left Danny, and he didn't look too keen on answering the question. He shrugged. "Live with my aunt and uncle. Older sister, but she doesn't pay me any mind."

"What happened to your parents?" Jack asked, making the others glad they didn't have to.

Danny peered up, his cheeks splotchy. "This is stupid."

Magpie felt a coolness wash over her, and she understood. His parents were both dead. From the messages she was receiving, his father had committed suicide, and his mother later died in a car accident. Both when he was little. His mother was clinging onto her living life, so she couldn't move on.

Magpie changed the subject. "If no one comes by tomorrow midday, we need to decide when to cut our losses and go out on our own again."

"I don't know, Magpie," Chase said, challenging her for the first time. "We're out of flares, low on food, and don't know where we are. Shouldn't we stay put until someone comes to find us?"

"What if no one comes?" Danny asked.

Magpie nodded. "That's the risk. We did what we could, but no one may have seen the flare and know we are here. We'll run out of food if we just sit around. We can follow the sun and keep moving south. Eventually, we have to hit something."

"Like a bear," Jack replied, only half joking.

They bedded down around the fire as the stars appeared

75

in the sky. They could make a decision in the morning. For now, they needed to conserve their strength and rest. However, the skies had other plans. The teens were jolted awake by a heavy downpour, which included large hail. It felt like rocks were being thrown at their heads, and they jumped up, running for the only shelter around.

The institution.

Magpie knew it was a bad idea, but the forces were making sure they had no choice in the matter. The kids scrambled through the blinding rain and pelting hail, grasping each other's hands so they all made it to the building. Donita led the way and ran to the large wooden door. She shoved hard on it as she pressed the latch. To their collective surprise, the door swung easily open.

Too easily.

As they tripped over each other through the opening, Magpie felt something grab her from behind and whipped around. Tyler was standing in the rain, not getting wet, his eyes filled with fear. He knew what she knew. They were being lured inside by forces that had no good intent. He shook his head at Magpie to let her know he wouldn't be able to go in. She paused, glancing at the others, now shaking the rain out of their hair and skin. She stepped back into the door threshold and stared at Tyler as they communicated.

"What should we do?" she mentally asked Tyler.

"You can't stay in there for long, Magpie. You won't get back out," he warned. "The longer you are in there, the stronger the hold on your mind. On the other children's minds. You might be able to fight it. At least, initially. They won't. They don't have the ability or strength to save themselves. Stay by the door!"

Point taken. Magpie had been taught to recognize and fight the unseen, but the rest of them had no idea what they were up against. Magpie needed to tell the others they had to stay as close to the door as possible, so as soon as the rain let up, they'd be able to go back out to the camp area.

If the rain let up.

Like Tyler, she knew this wasn't an act of nature. Not only were the dark spirits hungry to feed after so many decades trapped there, they knew what she'd done to her grandpa. They wanted revenge against her for what she'd attempted to do.

There was something she hadn't told the other teens. Not only was her grandpa aligning with the occult for his own desires to get what he wanted. That wasn't the main reason she'd tried to kill him. Not even that he was willing to sacrifice her to get what he wanted. There was a much bigger reason, one that could change the course of everything. He'd become their leader that night when they saw what he was willing to do. She turned to warn the others not to go further into the decrepit structure.

However, they were already gone.

CHAPTER 10

B ack at the second checkpoint, Brandi and Junior huddled around Cara, not sure what to do. The girl's fever had risen, and she was incoherent, mumbling about some guy named David as far as they could tell. They tried to speak to her, however, she didn't register that they were there with her. They hadn't heard from the others, and no one seemed to be out looking for them. Since the others hadn't come back yet, they feared the worst happened.

Junior stared off into the forest. "Maybe I should go back down the way we came. See if I can find someone."

Brandi shook her head. "You're not leaving me here, Junior! I'm sure the others found help and are on their way back to get us."

Junior didn't tell her, but he was sure they weren't. Earlier that day, he had gone to relieve himself and saw a woman standing in the forest. She had long white hair and was watching him. He called out to her, but she faded away like a cloud in the wind. He'd frozen, staring at the spot, then considered she had simply been the sunlight through the trees. The hair standing up on his arm told him otherwise, however, he didn't want to think about it.

Until now. The sun was going down, and no rescue was in sight. He felt like the woman was warning him of something. She seemed familiar, but he knew for sure he'd never seen her before. The more he thought about it, the more he understood the warning wasn't for him.

The other teens were in trouble.

Brandi lay down next to Cara and was humming a song to the incoherent girl. Cara seemed to respond and had stopped whimpering for the moment. Junior got up and stepped out of the rudimentary structure to look around. Brandi eyed him as he raised his hand to assure her.

"I'm not leaving. I'm just taking a walk to stretch and see if I can signal anyone with the flashlight. I'll be right back. I promise."

She smiled and closed her eyes. Junior paused as the image of Craig grabbing her near the ledge crossed his mind. Craig would've killed her. He would've killed all of them. But why? He didn't know any of them and had been a guide with Wilderness Reset for countless other excursions with no issues. They even had his picture on the website, smiling like a camp counselor.

Junior rubbed his temple and walked to the edge of the camp area. Everything about Craig had seemed off from the beginning, but Junior hadn't known that was a red flag. He thought Craig was simply discombobulated because the other guide hadn't shown up, and he was stuck with a rowdy group of teens by himself.

Why hadn't the other guide shown up? Initially, they were given the names of two guides. One male, Craig. One female, Katie. This was so Wilderness Reset could make sure male and female attendees had a safe person of their gender to ensure no inappropriate behavior happened. Katie hadn't shown up, but Craig insisted on going, anyway, without her. In hindsight, the teens should have refused to go then. However, they'd been treated like criminals up to that point and didn't know they could defy authority.

Junior thought back to how it all unfolded. All of the teens' families had received an email from Craig personally with the date and time to meet up to begin the hike. At the time, it didn't seem odd since they were already told he'd be their guide, but the more Junior thought about it, the stranger it became. The emails didn't come from Wilderness Reset, they came from Craig's personal email. Being their listed guide, it didn't set off any alarms. It coming from his own email was what made it out of the ordinary. None of them knew how it all worked, so they didn't think to question it.

That and he fumbled over their names when he called roll. He got Danny's wrong, forgot Junior's last name, and didn't even have Magpie on the list. Everything about it now made sense. Craig had ill intent from the beginning. Why? Junior couldn't figure that part out, however, he knew they weren't supposed to be there then. Something happened between Craig and Wilderness Reset to cause him to go rogue, then he decided to take it out on the teens for some reason. Craig didn't even know any of the teens before that day. They were simply assigned to him as wards for the original hike they were supposed to take.

A crime of opportunity.

Junior walked the perimeter of the campsite, flashing the light into the woods. As it got darker, if anyone was even close, they should be able to see the flashing light. He didn't know Morse code, but didn't think it mattered. He needed to get someone's attention, not send them a particular message. He paced back and forth for a while, clicking the flashlight. Realizing he might lose the battery, he clicked it off and wandered back toward the structure.

A scream cut through the dark, and Junior ran toward the sound. A figure of a man darted from the structure and disappeared into the woods. Junior considered running after him, but Brandi was freaking out inside. He squatted and dove in, peering around to see what happened. Brandi was pressed against the back of the structure, her arms clutched around her chest.

Junior shook his head. "Who was that?"

Brandi's eyes grew wide. "You saw him? You saw Craig?"

Craig? Craig was dead. Junior was confused. "I saw a man leaving the structure. He ran into the woods."

"It was Craig. I swear it," Brandi insisted.

"It couldn't be. He's dead, Brandi. We saw his body down at the bottom of the cliff," Junior countered.

She shook her head and pointed out, her hand shaking. "Junior, I saw him. He came in here. He was grinning in this creepy way. His eyes were black, empty. He was coming at me, his mouth all twisted like. I screamed, then he ran when he saw you coming back."

Junior sat down, his mind reeling. What if Craig wasn't dead? What if he survived and knew what they did to him? He closed his eyes and could see Craig lying at the bottom of the cliff, his head and body twisted in a way Junior was sure he was dead. There was no way Craig had survived that fall. If he hadn't, then who was that running from the structure? Who had Brandi seen? She was positive it was Craig.

A darker thought crossed Junior's mind, but he shoved it away before it took hold. He moved next to Brandi and put his arm over her shoulder. "We are tired, hungry, and disoriented. Our minds are playing tricks on us is all."

Brandi pushed him away and glared at him. "The same trick on both of us? I know what I saw, Junior."

He didn't doubt her, but couldn't risk it staying in his mind. He sighed and nodded. "I'll stay right here until morning. By then, hopefully, the others will bring back help. Close your eyes for a bit. I'll keep an eye out."

Brandi wiped her eyes with the back of her hand. He realized she'd been crying. She leaned against him and yawned. "I don't think I'll sleep," she murmured.

Despite saying that, she dozed off within a few minutes. Junior kept an eye out as promised, but the outside area remained quiet. A few times, he felt himself falling asleep and jerked awake. One of the times, he swore he saw Craig standing on the other side of the camp with a twisted grin like Brandi had described. Every time after that, when Junior found his eyes closing, he'd see Craig a few steps closer. Terror gripped him, and he forced his eyes to stay open.

He began to feel delirious, and the thought from before crossed his mind again. He knew Craig had died in the fall, but he also knew that *was* Craig watching them. Waiting. He was dead, but he wasn't done with them. He was biding his time to finish whatever he'd come to start. Junior couldn't stay awake forever, and Craig knew that.

Cara cried out in her sleep and mumbled, "Close your eyes, get a surprise."

Junior stared down at her as she smiled in her fever dream. *Close your eyes, get a surprise.* Craig was waiting for Junior to close his eyes so he could cross the gap between them. He couldn't let that happen. Craig was dead, he couldn't hurt them, Junior reasoned. Scare them, yes. Hurt them, no.

Or could he?

Sometime after midnight, Junior shifted Brandi down to rest next to Cara. His legs had fallen asleep, and he needed to move. He knew he couldn't go far, in case Craig was waiting for Brandi to be alone. He eased out of the opening and stood up, stretching his back. The campsite seemed benign, the fire coals burning strong. Junior stepped off to relieve himself and peered around. Nothing seemed off. He glanced back at the structure, which was quiet, as well.

He clicked the flashlight on and shined it around the

space, catching the reflection of a pair of eyes in the trees. Junior startled, then realized it was only an owl. Thinking about the talisman Magpie had given him that he'd smeared his blood on, he walked over to where he'd laid it on the ground. It was on the outside of the campsite, right where he left it. Too far. Craig had come in the other way, across from where the stone was.

Junior placed it outside the structure to protect the girls and went to the fire pit. He stoked the coals, throwing a few branches on top. The brighter the area, the more comfortable he felt. The fire began to rage, and Junior sat down beside it, still close to where the girls were resting. He needed to sleep, but he couldn't risk it.

He leaned his head forward onto the back of his hands, which were propped up with a stick from stoking the fire. *Close your eyes, get a surprise.* He snapped his head up and shook out the fogginess. He could sleep in the morning. Forcing himself to stay awake, Junior saw the colors of the sky begin to change, signaling daybreak was coming. He still had about an hour before the first rays of the sun would crest the horizon, and he was already bleary with exhaustion.

When he saw the man coming out of the woods, Junior tried to jump to his feet to stop him. Instead, he stumbled and almost pitched face-first into the fire. The man rushed toward him, grabbing Junior by the arm violently. Junior tried to take a swing at him, but lost his balance and tumbled to the ground.

"Whoa there, kiddo. You're alright. I'm one of the rangers who's been out looking for you. Wilderness Reset let us know you were out here and in danger. Settle down. You're okay now. Where are the rest of the kids?"

Junior stared up into a friendly face and began to cry. He gestured to the structure. "Sick. Cara. Fever."

The ranger frowned and rushed over to where the girls were sleeping to check on them. He called on his radio, too muffled for Junior to understand. Within a few minutes, the area was flooded with rangers, and they were loading Cara out. They asked him about the other missing teens. Junior explained they had gone to the next checkpoint for food and possibly to find help.

Brandi was now wide awake and talking to a female ranger. Junior was escorted to a large ATV with seats and a back that made it look like a little truck. He scooped up the talisman, slipping it into his backpack, and climbed into the bed of the ATV to lie down, knowing he could finally rest. The sound of the rangers talking was soothing, so Junior let his guard down. They were safe.

At least, *some* of them were.

CHAPTER 11

Magpie stood frozen, gazing into the dark building. She took a tentative step into the inky nothingness and whispered, "Chase, where did you go? Hello?"

Silence greeted her. Had they gone farther into the space? Against her better judgement, she continued forward, attempting to let her eyes adjust to to lack of light. Hearing noise to her left, she turned and followed the sound, however, ended up lost in the series of blackened hallways. It made no sense that the others would have just wandered off into the abandoned building like that. Especially because they didn't even want to go inside in the first place. Something must have lured them in. She'd only turned to communicate with Tyler for a moment, hardly enough time for the other four to simply vanish. None of it made any sense.

Tyler. She stopped and closed her eyes, calling to him. She knew he couldn't cross the threshold, but was hoping they could still communicate within the walls. Instead, the sounds of wailing and suffering filled her senses as the connection to the other world was bridged. She broke the connection and gasped. This place was bad. Where human cruelty and demonic forces joined together. They needed to get out as fast as possible.

Where were the other teens?

Magpie turned back the way she came, but it was as if the walls had shifted, changing the layout. Instead of taking her back to where she'd come from, she found herself lost in a series of pitch black halls and doors. Magpie began shoving doors to rooms open to cast light from the windows inside. The light illumination of the hallway gave her pause.

Strange drawings covered the walls, and it didn't appear like kids had done them. Like cave drawings, they seemed to tell a story. A terrifying story of torture and evil. Magpie could feel the sensation of hands touching her and shuddered. She knew they weren't in physical form, even so, she could tell they were of ill intent. Wanting to use her powers.

Protecting herself with the spell her mother taught her when she was a young girl, Magpie pushed farther into the space to find the others. The forces there wanted them to be separated to create weaknesses among the group. They were stronger together, and the haints knew this.

As she walked past rooms, she could see what happened in each one. People tied to beds, starved, denied care, and dying in their own waste. People who were already vulnerable because of their conditions. Even children. What she'd learned growing up with the abilities shared from generation to generation, was human suffering opened portals to other worlds. Some kind, some cruel. When humans caused suffering on one another, it was almost always the cruel forces that came through, as they fed off the evil of humans. People caring for others' suffering brought forth more gentle spirits.

Magpie stopped to listen out for the other kids. Her ears strained for any sounds of life, however, the spirits used this to get into her head, whispering her name and creating doubt. She was used to it, though, and shut them out. She knew the other teens didn't have that ability and could easily lose their sense of reality in a place like this.

Lose their minds.

She came to a door at the end of the hall and tried to open it. It was locked. Pressing her ear to the door, Magpie listened for anything on the other side. She swore she heard Chase's voice and knocked. As if something was moving across the floor, dragging a heavy object behind it, Magpie could tell there was a presence in there, but not a human presence. Fear squeezed her heart, and she knew she needed to run. The door handle rattled as if it were being unlocked, causing Magpie to stumble back. Whatever was about to open the door was not of that Earth.

Magpie ran down the hall as fast as she could, tripping over her own feet. She came to a stairwell going up. Despite everything in her telling her no, she bolted up it anyway. It led to another floor, with another hall, with more doors. Magpie paused to hear if she was being followed, however, the building had once again fallen silent. A shadow moved across the hall up ahead, and she narrowed her eyes to make it out. This time, it seemed human. Magpie crept along the wall, staying in the dark spots not touched by light. She made it to where she observed the shadow and saw an open door.

Afraid to speak, Magpie pushed the door open more and gazed in. A figure was standing by the window with its back to her. Tuning into her senses, Magpie got the sense the figure was human and called out, "Who's there?"

The figure whipped around and barreled toward the door. Toward *her* at an alarming rate of speed. Magpie stepped back as the door flung open and the figure tackled her. Trying to catch her breath, she rolled away, pressing herself against the far wall. The figure stumbled to its feet, looking around for her. Magpie was grateful for the shadows as she tried to regain her bearings.

The figure crouched down, staring in her direction. She was just about to flee out of the room when she heard a familiar voice. "Magpie, is that you?"

"Chase?" she squeaked out.

"Yeah, it's me."

She jumped up and flung her arms around Chase, knocking them both over. He grunted and reached out, touching her face. "Thank God it was you. I was freaking out."

"How did you get up here?" she asked.

"I don't know. We ran inside and were standing near the door. Jack thought he saw a light down the hall, and we went to see what it was. Like a lamp or something. When we got there, there was no light. We turned to go back to the door outside, but it was gone. So were you. We ended up lost in a series of halls and stairs. It seemed like every time I looked around, another one of us was gone until it was just me. I was looking out the window to see if I could climb out and down, however, they are all sealed shut. Have you seen the others anywhere?"

Magpie shook her head. "No. I turned, and you were all gone. Same thing happened to me. I got lost and couldn't find my way back to the door out. We need to find the others before..."

"Before what?" Chased asked softly, his brows drawn down in worry.

"I don't know. I guess, before someone gets hurt," Magpie answered, not wanting to say by what.

Chase peered around. "Do you have a flashlight or anything on you?"

"No. My batteries are dead. You?"

"Same. It's almost like this place has energy that sucks power out of things," Chase said with a woeful chuckle.

"It does."

"What do you mean?"

Magpie sighed, knowing she had to tell him at least part. "I can't tell you everything, but I have like this sixth sense that lets me know the intent of a place. This place is bad. Haunted by things that occurred here, even before this building existed. Dark spirits, evil humans, things like that. We shouldn't be here, but I can't find the way out."

Chase listened without judgment and nodded. "I don't have a sixth sense, but I swear I felt things touching me, following me. Is that what you're talking about? What even is this place?"

"It was an institution where people with physical and mental disabilities were sent when their family and doctors didn't want to deal with them anymore."

Chase rubbed his face, his deep red hair falling over his eyes. "Damn. How do you know all of that?"

Magpie shrugged. "For one, look at it. Two, I've heard the stories."

She didn't mention they were from a ghost.

"Oh yeah, I forgot you were from around here. So, what do we do now?"

"We need to find the others, then find our way out," Magpie replied, not convinced it was possible. "We have to stick together, this place wants to isolate us."

"So I've seen," Chase replied. "Here, I have some rope and carabiners. Let's connect our packs together, so if something happens, we can't be separated from each other."

Theoretically.

Magpie knew the power the spirits had and didn't doubt they could pull them apart if they wanted. Even so, it brought her comfort to be attached to Chase. They fastened the rope and clips to their backpacks and began exploring the halls. Each room was empty, except for rusty beds and stained mattresses. Some rooms had what looked like torture devices, but Magpie wasn't sure her brain wasn't just playing tricks on her. Or the haints. Fear was their energy. They made it to the end of the hall and found another stairwell, this time going down.

Chase turned to Magpie. "Should we go down?"

"I guess so. I don't think anything is on this floor."

They eased down the stairs, listening out for the others. It led to another door, so they pushed it open. Magpie almost ran into Chase's back as he froze in place. She peered around him and saw why. They were in some type of medical facility. A surgery of sorts. She moved around him and tuned in to understand the purpose of the space. Images of people being operated on without anesthesia came to her mind. Screams, blood, death. They'd been experimenting on the patients in there. She began to shake and backed up.

Chase put his hand on her back. "What is it?"

"I can't tell you."

"Can't or won't?" he asked in a whisper.

Magpie didn't answer, and Chase understood. They crept through the space, careful to avoid touching any of the gurneys or instruments in their way. The more they went into the space, the more Magpie was inundated with the horrifying images. She picked up the pace, trying to get to the other side, which seemed to have a door out.

Once they reached the door, Magpie leaned over and vomited, not being able to escape the horror she was immersed in. Sensing her distress, Chase came forward and pushed on the door. It flung open, and they were in another room. A morgue. Magpie shook her head and turned around, but the door in was gone. They needed to move forward.

Magpie saw something move behind one of the tables and frowned. It was too small to be one of the other teens, however, it looked like a person. A young child. She could feel the child was a ghost with no bad intent. She tipped her head and opened her mind to speak to it telepathically.

"Hello. I'm Magpie. Are you alright?"

The child, a girl of about six, came around the side of the table, limping. Her legs were twisted and malformed. The girl walked on them as if she were walking on gnarled branches. "Hi. I'm Emily."

"Are you trapped here in this building?" Magpie asked.

Emily nodded. Quite often, ghosts were trapped where they died, especially if they didn't have loved ones to send them on their way. Magpie glanced at Chase, who was watching her with a funny expression. He could see she was detached from their current state. She had no choice but to tell him what she saw.

"There is a little girl here named Emily. I think she was one of the residents of this place," Magpie explained.

Chase's eyes grew wide as he took a step back. "Can she hurt us?"

Magpie shook her head. "No. She is a caught ghost. Not alive anymore, but unable to move on."

"Oh, why is she here?" Chase asked, still unsure.

"She needs our help."

CHAPTER 12

"**H**ow can we help her?" Chase asked, peering around for the unseen ghost.

Unseen, at least to him. Magpie eyed the girl and shrugged. "She hasn't told me yet. However, she probably knows the layout of this place and might be able to assist us in getting out of here."

Chased tipped his head. "She would do that for us?"

Magpie frowned with a laugh. "Ghosts aren't spooky like most people make them out to be. At least, not the majority of them. There are a few who are frustrated with their situation and lash out, but that is not the norm."

"Why do people act like they are, then?"

"I think most people don't know the difference between a ghost and, like, a haint or dark spirit," Magpie explained. "Those were never humans like ghosts were. Or not directly. They can inhabit weak or willing people open to their powers at times."

"Open how?"

Magpie saw Emily leaving the room and gestured to Chase to follow. "Come on. She wants us to go with her. Open like if they want to be powerful or are greedy, have bad intentions."

"Like murderers?"

"Depends. Some people murder out of frustration or misguided passion. The people who murder out of a sense of satisfaction or joy are open to those spirits and demons. But also not just murderers. Anyone who is willing to cause harm for their own desires is open like that," Magpie answered, moving behind Emily so she didn't lose sight of the child.

Chase fell silent, considering what she was telling him. Emily led them through a series of halls and large open rooms before coming to stop outside a closed door. She turned to Magpie and pointed with her hand toward the door. Magpie stared at the worn wooden door and cocked her head, not understanding. She reached out and tried to twist the handle, but it didn't budge.

"What's happening? What's in there?" Chase asked.

"I'm not sure, but she wants me to go in there. It won't open," Magpie answered, letting go of the handle.

Chase tried throwing himself against the outside of the door, but it was sealed tight. "Maybe we can find a tool or something to pry it open."

As he said that, they heard movement behind them and whipped around. It was coming from down the hall, and Chase froze in place, his eyes wide. Magpie felt a cold rush wash over her and shook her head. "We need to go."

"Why? What is it?" Chased questioned, his voice shaking in fear.

"I don't know, but whatever it is, it doesn't want us getting in that room. Let's move, we'll come back later."

"If we can find it again," Chase pointed out.

Magpie would take that risk. Whatever was coming down

the hall was angry at their presence and would do whatever it took to stop them. They ran down the hall the other direction, Magpie making mental notes on how to get back. She paused to reach in her pack and take out a flint, marking a large X on the wall to mark it for future reference. They ran up a stairwell and shoved a door open at the top, finding themselves in a dark space. She felt along the wall to try and understand what type of space it was. There didn't seem to be any windows. She bumped her head and realized they were at the top level of the building and the ceilings sloped down, which is where she hit her head.

The attic.

There was only one window at the far end, covered in slats. Magpie groped along the wall until she got to it and tried pushing the slats open. Chase came up beside her, and together they were able to get the slats to move a little to let light in. They turned around to view the space. It was a long room that ran the length of the building. Staying where the light cast its glow, the pair moved along the room floor. There were trunks and personal effects Magpie sensed were taken from the residents. She ran her hands across the surfaces, feeling the vibrations of suffering coming off of them.

She heard Chase gasp and glanced over. He was holding a blanket in his hands and was staring down at something. Magpie walked over to where he was standing and saw what caused his reaction. Under the blanket was a pile of bones. Human bones of all sizes. She reached down and placed her hand on the pile, closing her eyes. They'd all been murdered in the building.

She stood up and sighed. "These were patients here."

"What? Why are their bones up here? They died, and they didn't bury them? That's weird," he questioned.

"Because they didn't just die. They were killed. I guess when they closed this place, they didn't come up here and find these. The institution was shut down due to abuse back in the nineties."

"How do you know that?"

"I have my sources," Magpie replied, referring to Tyler. "Apparently, my great-grandmother tried to burn the place down to stop them."

"Really? Did you know her?"

Magpie shook her head. "No, she died the day she tried to burn it down. She stopped it, though. The blaze brought the fire department out, who then called the police. There were only a few survivors. They have all died since."

"What about the people who worked here? Did they go to prison for what they did to the patients?"

"I actually don't know. I only know about Margaret, my great-grandmother. I assume they were arrested when the authorities came out and found out what was going on." An unexpected wash of cold air came over them, and Magpie grabbed Chase's hand. "We aren't alone. No matter what, don't trust anything you hear or observe."

Chase clung to her hand and took a step back, afraid of what he couldn't see. Magpie settled herself and drew on the power within her to tune in to what they were facing. Her breathing regulated as she began to see with her third eye. In the room, she could make out a shape in the center. Not a human form, but still formed. It watched her with ire, understanding who she was. All of a sudden, it cackled and drew closer. Chase couldn't see it but sensed the change in her demeanor.

"Magpie?"

"Shhh, it's here. It feeds off fear and anger, so try to focus on something positive," she instructed.

It didn't make sense. Light was coming through the slats, so it must be daytime still. Haints were known to only come out at night. Yet, there it was in front of her, plain as the day it couldn't inhabit. It made her question to reality of the building itself and if they'd been drawn into a different plane of existence. Or if it was all a mind trick.

Chased shook his head and closed his eyes, doing his best to be anywhere but there. Magpie stepped in front of Chase, still holding his hand. The entity came right up to her, leaning over her. She refused to be intimidated and stuck her chin up in defiance. Confused and not used to a human pushing back, it set its sights on Chase. Magpie tried to block it, however, it used its ability to disperse around her and come together to get to Chase's side. His eyes were still closed, but he was trembling.

"Mama?" he whispered.

Magpie knew the spirit was getting into Chase's head. She turned and wrapped her arms around the boy tightly. "That isn't your mother. It's a haint. It's trying to use your vulnerability against you. Chase, stay strong."

Chase quaked in her arms as he lifted his free hand toward the entity. "I miss you so much, Mama. Daddy isn't the same without you. I want you to come home."

Magpie knew she needed to pull him back before it took over his mind. She let go of his hand and slapped him as hard as she could. "Chase!"

He recoiled but still seemed to be trapped by the creature. Magpie shook him and moved between the form and Chase. It drew back, knowing it couldn't control her. Chase buckled at the knees and went to the ground. Magpie would run out of energy to resist before too long. She closed her eyes and called on ghosts still caught in the building to help.

The air in the room shifted, and the coolness abated. Magpie opened her eyes and saw the entity retreating as wisps of smoke seemed to surround it. The wisps formed, and Magpie watched as some of the residents of the former institution encircled the creature.

She reached down and shook Chase. "We have to go."

He came to and peered up at her, his eyes filled with fear. He couldn't see what she could, but trusted her as she helped him to his feet and guided him out of the attic space. They stumbled down the stairs, back to the prior floor. Not sure what to do, they wandered through the halls, searching for the others and a way out. Chase was oddly silent, and Magpie understood that once an entity gets into someone's brain, it causes a rift in memory. Chase truly believed he was seeing his mother. It was a lot to process.

Exhausted, they sat down and ate some of the food they had on them, saving a little in case they found the others. If they didn't figure their way out, they'd eventually become dehydrated and possibly even starve.

Chase finally spoke, his voice faint. "Do you think we will ever get out of here?"

Magpie nodded as a protective need to shield him took over her. "We will. We need to find the other kids first, though. I am their only chance of getting out."

Chase chuckled dryly, sounding more like his old self. "Cocky much?"

"Shut up. No, I can ask the ghosts to lead us out. I think they want us to set them free first, though."

"You can do that?"

Magpie shrugged. "Maybe. I can try. I think we need to get back to that room Emily showed me. It seemed important to her."

"What do you think she was trying to show you in there?" Chase asked.

"I'm not sure. Whatever it is, I think might be a tool to release them from this place," Magpie explained.

A rustling came from behind them, causing both to stiffen up. However, Magpie sensed it wasn't a threat and turned around. A shadow approached them at a rapid speed, and Magpie jumped to her feet as she was accosted by the figure. Pulling back, Magpie stared into a familiar face she was relieved to see again.

Chase got up and wrapped them both in his arms.

"Donita! I'm so glad to see you," he said with a grin as he held Donita back to get a better look at her. "Have you seen Jack or Danny anywhere?"

She appeared worse for wear. Her hair was a tangled mess, and she had a long, bloody scratch running down her left cheek. She kept glancing behind her as if she expected something to leap out and grab them. She shook her head.

"No, we got separated, right after Chase disappeared. First, you were gone, next was Chase. Then Danny and Jack. It was like this place was trying to drive us away from one another. I don't know what happened to them. I thought I was lost in here alone forever. I can't believe I finally found you. What if Danny and Jack are lost for good?"

"Don't worry, we'll find them," Magpie assured her, then reached out and touched Donita's scratched cheek. "What happened to you? You look like you got hurt. Did you encounter anything strange when you were on your own?"

Donita nodded, her eyes brimming with tears. "Something attacked me."

CHAPTER 13

D onita stared off, her eyes distant as she recalled what happened to her. "Every time I turned around, another one of us was gone. Once I was alone, I knew I wasn't."

"Alone?" Magpie asked.

"Yes. Something was following me. Hunting me. At first, I thought Jack was messing with me because I'd feel something touch my back, but when I looked, nothing was there. After the first couple of times, I knew it wasn't Jack or another person," Donita explained.

Chase flinched. "What was it?"

Donita met his eyes, hers unblinking. "I don't know. It was tormenting me, which was bad enough to begin with, however, as time went on, it became more and more aggressive. Scratching me, pushing me... I could hear it in my head, laughing at me."

Her voice trailed off as she held up her arms. Long angry welts ran down her smooth brown skin. Chase reached out and touched one, his eyes filled with concern. Magpie chewed her lip, trying to decide how much she could tell them. How much trouble they were truly in. They were in danger, especially if they got separated again. This made her extremely concerned for Jack and Danny, hoping the two were still together. Donita began to sob softly and clasped her arms around her body.

Chase put his arm over her shoulders and looked at Magpie. "Tell her what you can see."

Donita frowned at Magpie. "What you can see?"

It was apparent she'd need to come clean, as it might be their only chance to get out of the building. "I have these, like, powers, um... abilities. I can see other planes."

"Planes. What?" Donita responded, her voice thick with confusion.

"Uh, like, other realities," Magpie treaded lightly. She didn't want to scare Donita off. Donita needed to believe her to trust her, and most people didn't.

"She sees ghosts and shit," Chase replied, wanting to speed the process along. "There's this little girl here, she can see, named Emily. She's been trying to help us."

Donita pushed his arm off her shoulder and glared at Magpie. "Don't mess with me right now, Magpie. I'm tired and don't need any other bullshit to deal with."

"I'm not," Magpie said, her voice shifting to firm and insistent. "Look, my family comes from a long line of people who can see beyond this world. It's not a gift. It's not a curse, either, but falls somewhere in between. I use it to understand things better, but it can also open doors to bad things."

"Bad things like what?" Donita asked, not totally believing what she was hearing.

Magpie sighed. They didn't really have time to get into all of it, but she needed to let them know enough to gain their trust. "Anything not human, or no longer in human form. So ghosts, demons, haints. Things like that. The thing is, once

104

you open the door, any of those can come through it."

"Are they here in this place?" Donita asked. "All of them?"

"You tell me," Magpie answered, letting Donita work that reality out for herself.

Donita touched the scratch on her cheek and nodded. "It tried to push me down the stairs. I could feel its presence as if a large man were standing behind me. When I was running and got to the top of the stairs, it became strong and shoved me. I stumbled but grasped the railing, so I didn't fall. I clung to it as I went down each step, feeling that thing's existence like breath on my neck. Once I got to the bottom, I began to run and saw you and Chase down the hall, praying it was really you and not another trick."

"Not another trick," Chase murmured as if he was trying to convince himself of that, as well.

"Do you still feel it?" Magpie asked.

Donita glanced around, then shook her head. "No."

Magpie knew it was because of her. As long as she stayed on the right side of intent, the haints would keep their distance. She hoped. She cleared her throat. "My grandpa? He decided he wanted to align with them."

"Align with who?" Chase inquired.

"So, there are different types of spectres. Ghosts, who were once human. Generally harmless unless they were bad humans, but even then don't have much power. Then there are demons, not of this world. They have a lot of power, however, they have a hard time using that directly against humans. Last are dark spirits, sometimes called haints, which are not of this world but also sort of are. They get into humans' heads and try to control them. People can live with dark spirits within them. They are the biggest risk because they can interact with humans and manipulate them."

"Your grandfather interacted with them?" Donita asked, surprised.

"Yes. See, humans that have the ability to interact with them can also control them through energy and certain spells. Get them to harm others," Magpie did her best to explain.

"That's why you tried to kill him?" Chase asked, a dawn of understanding crossing his face.

Magpie shrugged. "Yeah. He was going to do horrible things with that ability. He already had."

"What do you mean?" Donita questioned.

"You know when people talk about the angel and devil on your shoulder? Or people hear voices telling them to hurt other people?"

"Yeah?" Chase responded.

"Those things are real. They are haints. The dark spirits that float between worlds. They get into people's heads and make them do things like murder, rape, torture."

"Why would they do that?" Donita asked with a shudder.

"It gives them energy, it feeds them. Anyway, my grandpa was using them to gain power and harm his perceived enemies."

"Who did your grandfather see as his enemies?" Donita glared at Magpie, her eyes narrowing.

Magpie knew Donita was beginning to comprehend her meaning. "People not like him. People not like our family."

Chase was clearly lost and glanced between them. "Anyone care to fill me in?"

Donita stuck her arm next to Magpie's and stared at him. "See the difference?"

"No way?" Chase recoiled and looked at Magpie, not believing it.

She nodded, chewing her lip. "I had to do it, otherwise he would have hurt a lot of people. I'm not like him, I don't believe the things he does."

"He's not dead, though," Chase whispered.

"No. I failed, but I will finish this," Magpie answered, seeming much older than her thirteen years.

"Won't your family try to stop you? Why didn't they press charges?"

"They will and they didn't because we don't do that. The police pressured them to, but my family doesn't believe in turning on their own. So, they agreed to send me away."

"You turned on your own kind," Donita said flatly. "Aren't they mad about that?"

Magpie sighed. "I suppose, but the code is passed from generation to generation. If anything, they'll sacrifice me to the spirits."

Chase froze. "Sacrifice you? Like symbolically?"

Magpie laughed bitterly, shaking her head. "No. Like, not symbolically. They may have more to do with all of this than we know."

"This? Like being here?"

"That. Craig. Who knows? They have incredible powers. I don't think I'm meant to return home," Magpie answered. She glanced down the hallway. "We need to find Jack and Danny."

"Wait. You can't leave it like that. What do you mean by Craig?"

Magpie started down the hall, peering in each room. "Doesn't this all seem a little strange to you? The other guide never showed up. Craig was acting weird. He, uh..." She stopped, realizing they didn't know what happened.

"He what?" Donita asked, glancing behind herself as if she expected something to jump out and snatch her.

"Okay, I'm going to tell you something, I promised not to tell anyone. However, you need to know the truth. Craig didn't just fall. He was trying to hurt Brandi. Junior and I found them at the edge of the outcropping, and Craig was trying to take advantage of Brandi."

"Take advantage? Like rape?" Donita asked, horrified as the reality set in.

"Yeah. Then we heard him say he would kill her, so Junior

ran to stop him and Craig tumbled over the ledge," Magpie answered, softening the truth a bit. They came to the end of the hall and turned down another hall. Magpie marked the corner with the flint. "There's one more thing."

"Of course there is," Donita replied, her voice laced with frustration and exhaustion. "What?"

Magpie chewed her lip. "Lore says haints only come out at night. However, we have experienced them with light coming through the windows."

"Okay?" Chase asked. "What does that mean?"

"It means either the lore is wrong, or this place isn't on the same plane of existence we came from."

The other two remained silent, processing what she'd told them. At the end of the next hall, they arrived at a stairwell, and Magpie put her hand up to stop them. They needed guidance. She mentally called out to Emily for help. When she opened her eyes, Emily was blocking the entrance to the stairwell, shaking her head. They shouldn't go up there. Magpie understood and turned around.

"What?" Chase questioned.

"Emily says we shouldn't go there. It's dangerous. Let me ask if she has seen Jack and Danny." Magpie pictured Danny and Jack in her head, and Emily's eyes grew wide with recognition. The young girl nodded fervently. The others were in trouble. She moved past them and motioned for Magpie to follow her.

Magpie gestured with her head for Chase and Donita to come along. They were too freaked out to question it. Emily led them down a series of halls Magpie began to recognize, and goosebumps rose on her flesh. Emily was taking them to the room where Magpie heard the noises behind the closed door. The heavy dragging. Not much scared her, but whatever was in that room did. She didn't want to frighten the other two anymore than they already were, so she rubbed her arms and kept it to herself.

By the time they made it to the outside of the door, Magpie was trembling. Whatever was in that room, she wasn't so sure she could handle. It was demonic. She reached out and placed her hand on the door knob, feeling the dark energy radiating from behind the door. She could also sense a human presence in there. She couldn't make out if it was Danny or Jack but it was at least one of them for sure. She turned the knob, expecting it to be locked, but this time it rotated easily. She dropped her hand, not having the courage to push the door open. She had abilities, however, whatever was in there was much stronger than her.

Chase touched her shoulder. "Is it locked?"

She shook her head. "No. I don't think I can take down what's in there."

"What do you mean by take down? Is it a haint in there?" Donita whispered.

Magpie met their eyes. "It's some type of dark spirit. Maybe a demon, I'm not sure. It's very strong."

However, in addition to the sinister force, at least one of their teen companions was in there and in very real danger. She had no choice but to face what was behind the door. She called on her ancestors, feeling a different presence join her. She turned to see an older woman with long, white hair in a loose dress standing beside her. Immediately, she knew it was Margaret, her great-grandmother. The woman who'd tried to burn the building to the ground many years ago. The other two couldn't see Margaret and watched Magpie with confusion.

She reached out again and twisted the doorknob. The door swung open smoothly as if they were being invited in as guests to a party. What they observed inside the room caused Donita to scream and Chase to take a full step backward into the hall. However, Magpie knew she needed to go fully into the room, even though the sight before them caused her blood to run cold.

Jack was suspended in the air, his back arching unnaturally as blood streamed from his eyes. A creature of monumental proportions with long, bony arms outstretched turned to face the group at the door with a sadistic, pointed-tooth grin and fixed its blackened eyes on Magpie. She felt like a fly caught in a spider's web as it sized her up. It had been waiting all along for her.

"Welcome, child," it hissed into her soul.

CHAPTER 14

J unior woke with a start. He was drenched in sweat as they took the rescue vehicle back to town. Rangers had found them after Wilderness Reset put out a call that a guide had gone rogue and taken children into the forest unapproved. Craig hadn't responded when they asked him and the other guide, Katie, to check in. The expedition Junior and the others were supposed to be on had been cancelled when Katie was reported missing after the prior expedition. However, Craig didn't bother to let the families know that, rather taking the children anyway for his own purposes. By the time the families knew what happened, it was too late. The group was gone deep into the forest.

Katie's body was found later in the woods after a search went out for her, once her roommate alerted the authorities that Katie never returned home from the previous excursion. She'd been stabbed, but that wasn't all. *Bound and burned,* the rangers said to one another. The worst thing they'd personally seen in their time on the job.

Craig's body was found at the bottom of the cliff where the teens had last seen it. Now, knowing he'd been up to no good, Brandi and Junior told the truth about how he caught Brandi in the woods and tried to accost her, threatening to kill her. They left out the part of Junior shoving him over the ledge, saying Craig lost his footing when Brandi tried to get away and fell over the edge of the outcropping where they were. The rangers didn't seem surprised or accusatory, as Craig was the prime suspect in Katie's murder. The only suspect after the bloody bra was recovered from his belongings. Same blood type as Katie's.

Junior glanced around, seeing the signs of civilization. Roads, trails, markers. He tried to shake off the dream he had, but it sat in his gut like a greasy rock. Brandi was asleep beside him, and Cara was transported out by medics, having acute appendicitis it seemed. Junior and Brandi explained that the other teens went ahead to the next checkpoint for food to bring back, but hadn't yet returned. The rangers sent a crew ahead to gather those children and bring them to the ranger station. Now, Junior knew they wouldn't find them there.

He nudged Brandi awake. "Hey, Brandi."

She yawned and opened her eyes, looking less than pleased. "What?"

"I think the other kids are in trouble."

"Huh? Why?" She sat up and brushed the loose strands of hair out of her face as the vehicle bounced and rumbled toward the ranger station.

Junior felt slightly silly for what he was about to say, however, the feeling in his stomach said otherwise. "I had this dream. I guess it was a dream, but it didn't seem like it. This guy named Tyler in overalls told me they got chased into the woods by a bear and became lost. He said they went to shelter in this building during a storm."

"What building? Couldn't they get help there?"

Junior shook his head. "I don't think so. Tyler showed me the building in my mind. It looked like an abandoned school or something."

Brandi seemed intrigued by the dream but not convinced. "Junior, weird dream and all, but I sincerely doubt it's real. Who is this Tyler?"

"I don't know. He said he died a long time ago."

Brandi laughed. "Even weirder. So, a ghost came to you in a dream and said a bear chased the other kids into an abandoned school? Alright, then."

Junior could see he wasn't getting anywhere with Brandi and sighed. Now that he said it out loud, it did sound ridiculous. Maybe all the stress of the trip had invaded his dreams. He sat back in his seat and thought about the dream. It seemed important, like a message, but he was delirious with hunger and exhaustion. That could play tricks on the mind. He closed his eyes again and dozed off, this time with no dreams.

By the time they made it to the ranger station close to town, he'd pushed the feeling aside and was looking forward to going home and sleeping in his own bed. Cara had already been transported to the closest hospital. The rangers said she'd be fine once her appendix was removed and her fluids restored.

Brandi was asked to speak to police about what happened with Craig. Junior gave a statement as well, leaving out his part in all of it. Merely a witness to the encounter. As he sat with a cup of weak coffee and a granola bar, he felt the sensation of fingers on his neck and shuddered. The ranger sitting across the desk was on the radio, not paying attention, and no one else was around. Junior glanced behind him, his eyes landing on an old photo. He dropped the coffee, splattering the lukewarm liquid onto the floor and his feet. The ranger raised his eyebrows and hung up the radio.

"You alright, kiddo? Exhaustion getting to you? You're welcome to lie down on that cot over there to rest before your family comes for you."

"No, sir. Sorry, I didn't mean to drop it. I lost my grip. Can you tell me, who is that picture of?"

The ranger squinted at the wall. "Which one?"

Junior got up and walked over to the pictures. Some were of rangers, others looked like family members, however, that one was different. It showed a young man in military fatigues. He pointed to it. "This one."

The ranger joined him and peered at the picture. "Oh, if I'm correct, that was Ranger Wilson's family member, I believe."

"Can I speak to Ranger Wilson?" Junior asked in a shaky voice.

The ranger laughed and shook his head. "Not unless you have a time machine. Ranger Wilson died some years back. Pancreatic cancer. I think the boy in the picture was his uncle or something like that. Sad story, really. The boy died in the Vietnam War, and his father committed suicide after, story has it. Mother had already passed on, so the bank took the farm. Why do you ask?"

Junior bit his tongue. "Do you happen to know the boy's name?"

"I can't say as I do. I didn't work with Ranger Wilson much. He was on his way out as I was on my way in. I suppose we could take the picture down now, but I haven't thought much of it, to be honest." The ranger pulled the picture frame off the wall. It slipped out of his hand, shattering the glass on the floor. "Damnit. Guess old Hank is getting me back for taking down the picture of his uncle."

He went to the corner of the station and grabbed a dustpan and broom to sweep up the broken pieces. Junior reached down and picked up the wooden frame and picture, shaking the loose glass off. It seemed like the young man, a boy not much older than him, really, in the picture was staring right at him. He felt the sensation of fingers on his neck again and placed his hand on the spot where he felt it. The ranger cleaned up the shards of glass, depositing them in a trash can.

He stared weirdly at Junior. "Now, I know you don't know him, so what's your interest in the picture?"

Junior glanced up and shrugged. "Nothing, I guess. Just found it interesting."

"I see. Yeah, terrible time in this country. I was born about ten years after, but my mama told me about it. If you are into history or something like that, you're welcome to take it. I don't think Hank would mind. Not that he could say if he did," he joked.

Junior slipped the old photo out of the broken frame and went to slide it into his backpack when faded writing on the back caught his eye. He caught his breath when he realized what it said. He'd already thought the photo bore a striking resemblance to the ghost in his dream, however, the words clinched it.

"Tyler Randall 1949-1968. Gone but not forgotten."

Junior hid his shock from the ranger as the ranger asked more questions about the expedition and Craig. Brandi's family showed up a bit later, and she and Junior hugged as she got ready to leave. She gave him her number, and he promised to call. She waved with a smile as she climbed into her father's truck and didn't look back as they drove out of view.

Junior waited until the ranger stepped away and scanned the ranger station. He was about to get himself in incredible trouble, but he knew from the picture, his dream wasn't only a dream. It was a message. The other kids *were* in trouble. He found a set of keys in one of the desk drawers and slipped them into his pocket. His plans for Harvard might be getting dashed, but his desire to help the others was stronger. He found some packaged food and a couple of bottles of water, shoving them into his backpack.

About that time, the ranger came back in and eyed him. "Your family live far away?"

"Yeah, a few hours. Hey, I love abandoned places. Visit them as a hobby," he lied through his teeth. "Y'all have any around here?"

The ranger rubbed his chin. "Hmm, not that I can think of. There used to be this urban legend of a haunted mental asylum deep in the woods, but it turned out to be made up, I suppose. A story to keep kids from wandering into the forest, ya know? There are, like, old barns and some empty homes and all, but nothing too interesting. Trust me, if it existed, I would have seen it by now. I think we have covered about every mile of this forest."

Not every mile, Junior thought to himself. The place Tyler showed him didn't want to be found. Somehow, it had escaped notice. Junior looked at the clock on the wall and did mental math. If his family was notified when he first got there, possibly before, they'd be arriving soon. He had about six hours left of daylight and no more than an hour before he was being sent back home. If he was going to do something, he needed to do it now.

The ranger saw him looking at the clock. "Don't worry, son. They'll be here soon. I'm sure you are anxious to get back home and to your nice cozy bed after your ordeal. The police may still have some questions for you once you are home about what happened."

Junior's mind was spinning as he nodded. "I'm pretty tired. I guess I'll lie down until my family gets here if that's alright. I can use the cot?"

"Sure, sure. I'll step out so I don't disturb you. There's a blanket in that foot locker. I'll come get you when your family arrives."

The ranger gathered a few things and opened the desk drawer, causing Junior to freeze. What if he noticed the keys missing? Instead, he grabbed out a pack of cigarettes and smiled sheepishly at Junior as he tucked them in his pocket. "Don't ever start smoking, these things'll kill you."

Junior chuckled and lay on the cot. As soon as he was sure the ranger was out of sight, he gathered his pack, grabbed a map and compass off the desk, and slipped out of the station. The ranger was nowhere to be seen, so Junior crept over to the ATV and climbed on, praying the keys went to it. He tried different keys until one fit. He gently turned the key, and the engine turned over. Knowing the sound of the engine would draw attention to what he was doing, Junior gunned the engine and hung on as the ATV took off, haphazardly carrying him into the woods. He thought he heard yelling behind him, but focused on holding on and doing what he'd been led to do.

He had no idea where he was going, however, he was aware he wasn't alone.

CHAPTER 15

Magpie knew her abilities were not enough to take on the entity alone, but if she didn't do something, Jack would surely die. The entity had no interest in Jack directly, he was using the boy to lure her in. Like her grandpa, she sensed it wanted to use her abilities for its own purpose. She needed to allow it access to her so Jack would be let go, without sacrificing herself in the process. Something she didn't know how to control.

The others couldn't see the creature, but they could see Jack caught and twisting in the air. Chase and Donita clung to one another as Magpie moved farther into the room, careful to stay out of the entity's aura. That would trap her, as well. She scanned the room for Danny but couldn't see him anywhere. Pausing at the edge of the aura, she called out to Jack.

"Jack, can you hear me?"

The boy didn't respond, and she feared he might be too far gone already. She raised her hands as if she were about to play a piano and chanted softly, allowing her power to form an energy field around her. This would protect her as she moved through the aura surrounding Jack. Hopefully. She'd never done it for spirits of this magnitude. The energy around her formed into a bubble; she stepped into the aura, feeling it immediately drain her. The entity watched her with amusement as she fell to her knees. She wasn't strong enough to even protect herself, much less anyone else.

Margaret stepped in and created a counter-aura to shield Magpie. She couldn't fight the creature alone as a ghost, but she could summon a forcefield over her great-granddaughter for added protection. Magpie was frozen between the auras, not able to move forward or back.

Chase and Donita saw her crumple to the floor and knew whatever she was fighting was winning the battle. Chase glanced around the room, trying to understand where the force was coming from. Landing on a focal point, he stepped forward, appearing more sure of himself than he felt.

"Come and get me, you piece of shit!" he yelled in the direction he thought the entity might be. He was off, but his bravado distracted the creature. It turned on the boy, and Chase found himself being invisibly dragged into the center of the room. Donita grabbed his arm and held on, as they both were drawn inward.

Magpie felt her strength return as the spirit focused on its new prey. Margaret nodded at her with a mutual understanding. Magpie leapt to her feet and ran full force at Jack, jumping up to latch onto his ankle with her hands. This broke the connection, and Jack fell to the floor. The creature, realizing its prisoner had been released, whipped around with a roar. Magpie crouched over Jack's inert body, considering how she could get them all out of there, when something unexpected happened. Danny came flying out of a closet, screaming and waving his arms like a maniac.

It was almost comical, and the entity seemed thrown off

its guard. Chase ran forward and helped Magpie drag Jack to the door. Danny was on their heels as the spirit was sending a swath of webbed energy to try and catch them. They made it to the door, and Donita snatched Danny's hand as Chase and Magpie shuttled Jack through the opening. They slammed the door behind them, praying it was enough to keep the entity in there. Chase leaned over, trying to catch his breath.

"Can't it follow us?" he gasped.

Magpie shook her head. "I don't think so. I don't know why, but if it could have, it wouldn't have lured us in there. It must be trapped in that space."

"How?" Donita asked.

Magpie ran her hands along the door, feeling something unusual. What she felt wasn't visible to the naked eye, but she could feel the bumps on the door. Braille. It seemed to spell out something, but she didn't know how to read Braille. Even so, she understood. It was a spell to stop the entity from crossing the threshold. All it would take was something to break the spell to set it free. Or open the door.

She couldn't let that happen.

Margaret was gone, but Magpie understood she was still present in the building, watching over and protecting Magpie. They needed to move away from the door and find a safe place to rest to regain their strength. Magpie remembered seeing a room with symbols on the wall down one of the halls. Someone had created those to block out haints, she believed. They needed to retrace their steps.

"Can you carry Jack? There was a space that should protect us. I remember seeing it in one of the halls. I marked walls so we can follow the markings back to the space," she suggested.

Danny and Chase picked up Jack on either end and lifted him, but Jack's middle still dragged the floor. Donita stepped in the middle and braced Jack's midsection. That way, the three of them were able to move the unconscious boy while

Magpie led the way. They were losing daylight and needed to move quickly before they lost sight of the flint markings.

The hallways got dim as they crept along the walls, searching for the markings. By the time they went down a few halls and turns, it was almost pitch black. Magpie ran her hands along the wall, feeling for the marking. They couldn't risk being stuck in the halls in the dark as they would lose their senses and become vulnerable to the spirits lying in wait.

Her hand brushed a different texture, and she knew it was one of the flint Xs. They were close. Groping along the wall, she felt an opening and pushed on a door. Moonlight streamed into the room, and she knew they'd made it.

"Come on, in here. This is the space I was talking about," she whispered to the others.

They slipped into the room and shut the door behind them, sealing off the rest of the institution. Chase and Danny set Jack on the floor as Donita made sure he landed softly. Chase collapsed next to the unmoving boy, resting his hand on Jack's chest.

"Is he alive?" he asked Magpie.

Jack was in bad shape, but she could feel the energy of life in him. Barely, but it was there. She nodded. "He is, but he isn't out of the woods yet."

"Ha, none of us are," Donita answered bitterly. "We never should have come in this place."

Magpie knew what she meant. They were lost and trapped in a building that didn't want them to leave. She turned to Danny. "What happened? How did you end up in that room?"

Danny stared at her, his eyes pained. "We got lost in the maze of this place. Don't laugh, but we held hands after Chase and Donita disappeared, so we couldn't get separated. We came to that door, and it sounded like someone was inside there. We thought it was one or all of you, so we went in. At first, it seemed like any other room, but then the door slammed shut, we couldn't get out. We couldn't see anything in there, but there was a weird sound. Like a high-pitched hum. Jack started to convulse as this bluish light filled the room. All of a sudden, it was like Jack was possessed. He started moaning and thrashing. When he lifted into the air, I freaked out and hid in the closet."

"How long were you in there?" Magpie asked.

"I don't know. Maybe like thirty minutes or so? Seemed like forever. Jack was suspended in the air, then his eyes started bleeding. I didn't know what was causing it, but I was scared. I tried calling out to Jack. He didn't respond. I thought we were both dead for sure until you showed up."

Magpie understood. She was being called to that space by the entity. It knew she had to the power to release it from captivity. "Could you see what was holding Jack?"

Danny shook his head. "No, just that noise. Light and sound, nothing else. What was it?"

"An entity of some sort. It wanted me."

Danny frowned, not sure he believed her, yet couldn't deny what happened. "Why you?"

"Magpie can do magic," Donita replied.

"No, not magic. But I do have abilities. Powers that thing wants," Magpie explained.

"Why?" Danny asked.

"Because my powers can set it free. However, I have to be willing or forced. I guess it thought if I saw Jack like that, I would bend and set it free."

"Would you have? I mean, set it free to save Jack?" Chase chimed in, his voice almost accusatory.

Magpie understood his doubt. Clearly members of her family were willing. However, she was not. "No."

"What if it killed Jack?" Danny asked, definitely accusing. "You wouldn't have saved Jack?"

Magpie considered her answer carefully. "I know it's hard to understand, but had I set it free, I still wouldn't have saved

Jack. It would have killed us all. The only way to save Jack was not to save Jack by setting it free. I had to take that chance."

Danny didn't like that answer and turned away. Magpie couldn't blame him. Sometimes people were sacrificed for bad, but sometimes they were also sacrificed for good. Chase was watching her, his face unreadable. He seemed to understand what she was saying, even so. He pulled his knees to his chest and cleared his throat.

"So, would you let us all die to stop that thing from being let go?"

Magpie hated she was being put in that position by their questions. They didn't comprehend how powerful the spirits were. That one in particular. How if it took control of her powers, it would decimate everything in its path. They were thinking in human terms, she was having to fight outside of them. Now all eyes were on her, and she knew they wouldn't let it go.

"You know that question where they ask if you would let a single person tied to the tracks die to save a group of people tied on the other track if you were in charge of which track the trolley went on?" she asked.

No one answered her at first, but then Donita spoke up. "Yes. We talked about that in school. The teacher called it a moral dilemma."

"There is no correct answer, right? Either way, someone suffers. No matter what the choice is, the person making the decision is always wrong. They can't win. If they make one choice, they kill an innocent person; if they make the other choice, they kill many innocent people. In the end, they are the villain even though they didn't set the wheels in motion to begin with."

"Okay?" Danny said. "So?"

Magpie sighed. "If I set that entity free, it would destroy people. If I didn't, it would kill Jack. I can't make the right choice because there is no right choice."

Donita nodded as the understanding came. "Wait. So, why didn't it kill Jack? You didn't set it free."

Magpie cocked her head, seeing they didn't understand what happened in that room. The part they all played against the beast. "I didn't have to make the choice in the end, don't you see?"

"Why not?" Chased questioned.

Magpie leaned forward, meeting their eyes. "Because of you. The entity thought it had the game figured out. It against me. A battle between the two of us. I either had to sacrifice Jack's life to keep the spirit trapped, or give in and let it win to save him. It had the upper hand because I'm not strong enough to beat it."

"I don't get it. Then, why didn't it win?" Danny mumbled, trying to figure it out.

"You all fought back. You were the secret weapon it didn't see coming."

"What does that mean?" Chase asked, attempting to understand her point.

Magpie tipped her head and smiled. "You saved Jack."

CHAPTER 16

The teens had a fitful night of sleep, jumping at every sound. Even so, nothing came into the room, and they were able to let their guard down a little bit. Danny and Jack had lost their packs in the chaos of being trapped by an unseen force. Magpie considered them not being able to see what was after them probably saved their sanity to a degree. Donita and Chase had miraculously held onto their bags, and the group split the tiny bit of food they had left, except for a can Magpie set aside.

By morning, they were slightly rested and sat in a small circle to talk things through. Jack was still unconscious, but they made the circle to include his prostrate form anyhow. Magpie checked on him and could see he was breathing, but she didn't know what kind of internal damage the entity had done to him. Especially his brain. She pried open his eyelids, seeing his eyes were completely bloodshot, even though they had stopped bleeding. No white was visible. Even so, he was still alive.

"So, should we just stay in this room?" Danny asked, sitting close to Jack.

Magpie shook her head. "I think we're safe in here, but we need to try to get out of the building. To do that, we need to leave the room."

"Why?" Danny questioned. "If we are safe here, why don't we just stay put?"

"Because we'll starve to death if we never find a way out," Donita answered flatly, understanding their predicament.

"Right. We are out of food, and no one knows we are in here. I don't know if people know this place still even exists, to know to look for us here. If we don't leave and try to find help, we'll die inside these walls," Magpie added. She sympathized with Danny's desire to not go back out into the building and face what was waiting for them there, but it was their only chance of getting back to the outside world.

Chase listened, fiddling with the cord of his backpack. He chewed his lip. "What about Jack? We can't move him right now. He'll slow us down. I think he's safer in the room."

Magpie didn't disagree. They couldn't drag Jack through the halls with them, however, if they found their way out of the building, they might not be able to get back to him. Part of her knew their chances of finding a way out were slim. They were being tricked and misled. She needed to be able to communicate with any ghosts in the building to see if they could help. She suspected they couldn't come into the room, either, due to the symbols casting a protective spell on the space.

She needed to leave the room, either way.

"You all can stay here and I'll see if I can find an exit," she offered as a compromise.

"No, you can't go out there all by yourself," Donita insisted. She'd experienced what happened being alone and didn't want Magpie to face that.

Magpie showed a knowing smile. "I'm never alone. One of the benefits and curses of my abilities. I need to communicate with the others, but I can't do it in this room. I can mark the walls to find my way back here. The only way we'll get out of this building is to find the exit. I need help doing that."

"I'll go with you," Chase offered. "Maybe my mother can watch over and protect me."

Magpie didn't want to explain that his mother couldn't cross the threshold of a place she'd never been, so she nodded instead. "Alright. Chase and I will go. That way, Jack isn't left alone in case he comes to. I'd hate if he did and wandered out into the halls alone."

Danny seemed okay with that decision. Maybe out of his newly formed friendship with Jack, more likely out of fear. Donita glanced between them, trying to decide where she should be. Finally, she stuck her chin up with determination, her deep brown eyes glinting.

"I'll go with you and Chase. How do we make sure we don't get separated again, though?"

"Chase and I were using rope and carabiners to hook together. It seemed to work," Magpie explained. She twisted the ends of her fine, light-brown hair between her fingers and glanced toward the door. "We should use as much daylight as possible. Danny, stay with Jack, so if he comes to, you can explain everything to him."

Danny nodded, placing his hand on Jack's shoulder. "You'll come back for us, right?"

Chase smiled as he got up. "Leave no man behind."

"Leave no *one* behind," Donita countered and got up next to him. "Now or never."

Magpie was impressed by their courage, considering what they were up against. Although only she truly knew the expanse of it. They knew it was something like what they'd already experienced, she knew it was terrifying beyond worldly realms. She stood up and took out the can of green beans she'd set aside, then handed it to Danny. "Give this to Jack once he wakes up. He'll need to eat something. I saved it for him."

Danny took the can and met her eyes. They all understood they only had each other to depend on at this point, no matter how they ended up there. He slipped the dented can next to him. "Thanks, Magpie."

The three standing teens gazed at each other, trying to push the fear away. Once they left the room, they were back at the mercy of the institution and its unearthly inhabitants. They clipped their packs together so they hopefully wouldn't get separated. Nothing was guaranteed.

Magpie took a deep breath and led the way to the door. She turned back to Danny. "One more thing, Danny. Don't answer the door, no matter what."

Danny tipped his head. "Wait, why? What if it's you?"

"Because we won't knock when we come back and they will to make you open the door," she replied.

"They?" Danny asked, his eyes wide.

"Yes. Haints can't cross this spell with the door closed, but they will try to lure you out or cross the threshold. Opening the door to their knock might allow them to cross over the threshold. Do you understand?" Magpie questioned, waving her hand at the symbols all along the walls.

With the door open, the symbols were nothing more than that. Spell markings. It took multiple aspects to create the seal. The symbols had certain protective qualities, but likely not up against what was roaming those halls.

Danny scanned the symbols and shook his head. "I don't, but I believe you. I won't answer the door."

Magpie bobbed her head. "Even if it sounds like someone you know on the other side of the door. Don't answer it. We know to come in, so don't open that door, okay?"

Donita cleared her throat. "What if it's rescuers?"

"It won't be. They won't find this place," Magpie answered. "It's not on any map anymore. Like I said before, I'm not even sure it's visible to the outside world. We're here because it wanted us to be."

The temperature in the room seemed to drop, and they fell silent. If any of them had doubts about her abilities, they didn't now. Chase put his hand on the doorknob and met Magpie's eyes. She nodded and glanced at Donita. Donita shifted her backpack and gave a wary smile. Chase turned the knob and pushed to door open into the hall. It appeared benign, but they all knew better.

Once in the hall, they shut the door securely behind them and looked in each direction. Magpie called on the spirits and waited. Emily appeared at one end of the hall, and Magpie turned to the others. "This way."

"How do you know?" Donita asked.

"I have a guide. The little girl Emily is showing us the way. I need to tell you both something. Haints like to mess with people's minds. You may see or hear things that seem very real but aren't. Sometimes familiar things, like people you know. Sometimes terrifying things. Don't trust them. Only I, or anyone else with the sight, can see what's on the other side. Everything else is their concoction to break you down."

"Why do they want to break us?" Chase asked, fearing the impending answer.

"That's how they get stronger. The more we lose control of our minds, the more they gain control of them and feed off the energy. No matter how real something seems, it isn't."

The other two looked at each other nervously, and Magpie could see they were questioning their decision to come along with her. She had no way to reassure them everything was going to be alright because she didn't know if it would be. She paused and glanced back at the door they'd just come through.

"You can go back in there."

Chase shook his head and clutched his backpack, determined. "No. I'd never let you do this alone."

Donita appeared less sure, but began moving forward anyway. "This way?"

Magpie nodded, seeing Emily waiting for them at the end of the hall. "Yes."

As they walked through the halls. Magpie noticed something that made her feel less sure. The markings she'd made on the wall were now scrubbed away. Something didn't want them to find their way back to the room. Even so, she continued making the marks as they walked, pressing harder to score the wall. Danny and Jack needed her to come back and save them. She only hoped the new markings she made would stay put.

She doubted they would.

Emily led them through an old kitchen and paused by a door off the kitchen. Magpie let her know to allow them to stop for a bit. They scavenged through the cabinets, but any food was long gone, likely eaten by rats. Even if it hadn't been, she doubted it would be safe enough to eat all these years later. She checked her canteen and found it was less than half full. They'd need to conserve whatever water they had. Chase left his canteen with Danny, so they only had two partially full ones left between all of them.

They moved on through what appeared to be an old dining hall with large multi-paned windows. Each of the kids went to the windows and stared out at the forest just beyond their reach. Visible but inaccessible.

Chase turned to Magpie, a question in his eyes. "Can't we break the windows and climb out?"

She shrugged. "Seems too easy, but we can try."

Try, they did. They pounded on the glass, threw their backpacks at it, even tried smashing their metal canteens at the seemly thin glass, but nothing happened. Not a crack. Magpie suspected as much, but didn't want them to lose hope. Finally, exhausted, they stood watching the breeze gently move the leaves of the trees on the other side of the panes. A bird flew close to the window but didn't seem to register them on the other side of the glass.

Magpie saw Emily watching them with a sad expression on her small, round face. Like them, she was stuck there. Margaret had understood the institution was not only a prison for the living, it was a prison for those who'd passed on there. Only destroying the structure would release the ghosts. Magpie met Emily's eyes, and a look of mutual understanding crossed between them. Magpie would do her best to set the ghosts free.

If she was even able to set herself and her friends free. Friends. Something she'd never really experienced before. Her family insisted on schooling at home and kept everyone isolated from the outside world. They said it was for their safety, but now Magpie believed it was for something else. For control of their abilities. As she was considering this, she heard Donita gasp and spun around.

Donita had her hand to her mouth, pointing to the far end of the dining hall. Chase and Magpie followed her gaze, but there was nothing there. Nothing they could see, anyhow. As Magpie predicted, the haints were starting their mind games. Magpie went to touch Donita's shoulder when the girl fell to her knees, her eyes fixed on the thing her mind was seeing outside her body. Donita shook violently.

She began to scream.

CHAPTER 17

Magpie knelt next to Donita, wrapping her arms around the girl. She knew what Donita was seeing was very real to her, even though it was a mind cast. Touching Donita helped Magpie to see what the frightened girl was seeing. Her eyes followed Donita's terror-stricken gaze, and Magpie swallowed hard. Even though she knew it wasn't real, Magpie still felt the hair on her arms rise. On the far end of the room, strung from the rafters, were bodies. Bodies of women and children whose skin was brown like Donita's. Magpie faced her friend and tried to get Donita to look at her.

"It's not true, not real. They are getting into your head and pulling out your deepest fears," she insisted, shaking Donita gently. "Donita, look at me."

Donita's eyes barely tore away from the sight, then flitted to Magpie and back. She was entranced by the images, and not in a good way. Magpie put her fingers on Donita's chin and turned her face to her own, forcing Donita to meet her eyes.

Donita didn't blink, but she did look at Magpie. "How?"

Magpie dropped her fingers. "Keep your eyes on mine. They can read your thoughts, especially your fears. Those are not real people, they are projections. If you don't believe it, they will go away. Close your eyes and think of something hopeful. Your family, or your home."

Donita nodded slightly and let her eyes close. Her shoulders relaxed as tears slid from between her lashes. Magpie began to doubt letting them come along with her. She knew what to expect from the haints, and while she'd told them what might happen, seeing it in person was completely different. The images were as real as life to them. Or death, as it might be.

Chase came and squatted next to the two girls, not able to see what they were seeing. He glanced at Magpie, who kept her focus on Donita and drawing her out of the hypnosis. Donita let her eyes open a slit and peered back where she saw the hanging people. They were gone, the room was empty except for the three teens. She let out a long, ragged breath and rubbed her nose. Magpie helped her rise, and the three stood in place for a moment.

Magpie turned to Chase. "They will try with you, too, like when you thought you saw your mother. There is nothing here. This place has been abandoned for decades. Honestly, it might not even be a standing building anymore. That could have been a hallucination, as well."

"I don't understand," Chase replied, his brow knitted. "How are we in here, then?"

Magpie shrugged, not knowing how to explain. "Maybe we aren't."

The other two gazed around the space, not believing it couldn't be real. Chase stomped on the floor, kicking up dust. "Was it ever real?"

"Yeah. This was actually a place they sent people with mental and physical differences until the nineties. It was shut down for widespread abuse at that time. I don't know what happened after that. I do know it wants us here."

"Why?" Donita asked.

"Well, I guess it wants *me* here for sure. I believe you all were unintended passengers. It wants me like it wants my grandpa. We can set them free, I think."

"Them? The ghosts, or the haints?" Chase asked.

"All of them. The ghosts I want to set free, the haints not so much. Not at all, to be honest. I need to figure out how to get us out and not do that."

They moved toward the far end, where Donita saw the bodies hanging. Even though they were gone, she skirted the wall as if she were avoiding touching them. Chase frowned and stared at where her eyes were fixed. Not seeing anything, he walked straight through where their feet would have been. On the far side was a doorway with the door long gone. They went through it and paused.

Magpie looked for Emily, but she was nowhere in sight. The ghosts didn't like to intermingle with haints, so Magpie figured the haints were close by, waiting to get into Chase's head, as well. She looped her arm through his and whispered. "Be on guard."

He glanced down and nodded, understanding he was the next target. They inched down the hall, jumpy and cautious. After a few minutes, Emily reappeared to Magpie and motioned for her to follow. This meant the haints had given up for the time being, liking to strike when the guard was down. Emily led them to a door which seemed to lead to the outside, but when they tried to open it, the door wouldn't budge. It looked like a door, but felt like concrete to nowhere.

Magpie gestured for them to sit for a bit as she considered their options. The windows couldn't be shattered, the doors out couldn't be opened. She was missing something. At least, she knew where the door was now. They needed to go back for Jack and Danny and bring them to the door. *If* they could get back. It seemed like the building was in an ever-changing state, and she wasn't sure her markings would be where she left them anymore.

She decided to have a chat with Emily to see if she could gather more info. She needed to sit alone to do that, so she turned to Donita and Chase. "I need to step away for a minute. Stay right here, stay with each other. Hold hands if you have to, but don't go anywhere."

"Where are you going?" Chase questioned, not looking happy about her going elsewhere.

"I'm just stepping over there, still in eyesight. I need to talk to Emily and try to gather more info. We can't get out because there is something I'm missing. Something I need to do, but I don't know what it is."

Donita took Chase's hand. "Go do what you need to, Magpie. We'll stay right here. Whatever it takes to get out of this hellhole."

Magpie wandered over to an alcove. She sat down in it and summoned Emily to her. She felt Emily sitting across from her and opened her mind. "Emily, what am I missing? Why can't we get out of here?"

Emily smiled, and Magpie realized how beautiful the little girl truly was. Despite her deformities, she was lovely and had a kind, open face. A pure spirit. Emily spoke. "You were brought here to complete a task."

"Margaret? Am I supposed to finish what she started?"

"Miss Maggie? She was very kind. She volunteered here and sang us children's songs. She brought pastries. The others didn't like her, but couldn't very well tell her to leave."

Magpie liked how Margaret was called Maggie, she never knew that. "The others? The haints?"

Emily shook her head and began speaking well beyond her years. "No, the living. They were very cruel. Many people died here at their hands. At first, it was run like a home or a hospital. Everyone had a room that was clean, and they were fed. However, the original wards became tired of the workload and left. They were replaced with people who were less kind. This cycle continued until the people here seemed to enjoy causing suffering. This opened the gateway to the others. The haints. People died every day. Some of the wards committed suicide, too. Before long, there were few people and more of the others. The people in charge chained the living to beds, radiators, and pipes. Whatever they could find to stop the residents from moving. They stopped feeding everyone... people eventually starved to death."

"Where was Margaret?" Magpie asked, trying to understand how things could get so bad.

"She used to come to visit, then was gone for some time. Years maybe. I don't remember. Then, near the end, she came back. I had died by then. When she found out what was happening, she left to get help. She tried to take some of the living with her, but they were too weak. No one would listen to her. She came back and saw the place was overrun with the haints. The living were barely alive, and she knew she couldn't save them. She spoke with the living, they asked her to help them die. The only way to stop it all was to destroy the building. The haints were trying to figure out a way out to spread into the forest. A few did by latching onto the wards who left. However, they couldn't leave without a living one. Margaret knew this and knew the innocent living left would never leave. The remaining wards were planning to leave them behind and disappear into the forest."

"So, she was going to burn it all down. Them included... and herself?"

"Yes. She had the sight, like you. They want you now. If you leave, they will go with you into the forest."

Magpie now understood. They couldn't leave. Not without destroying the place and themselves. She was one thing, but the other teens hadn't asked for this. They were simply with her. She couldn't sacrifice them.

She thought about something. "Emily, who is holding the doors and windows shut, then?"

"The ghosts. They want to be free, but they know the costs," Emily explained.

Magpie chewed her lip. There had to be a way to set the ghosts free and the other teens. She remembered something and tipped her head. "The room you showed me? Is there something in there that could help? Is that why you showed it to me?"

Emily gazed off. "There are answers in there."

"Will they help?"

Emily snapped her eyes back to Magpie. "You tell me, Maggie."

Magpie jolted. Why did Emily call her Maggie? "I'm Magpie."

"Magpie, Maggie. One and the same."

Was she Margaret? Returned to finish the deed? No, because she and Margaret existed in the same space at the same time when they released Jack from the entity. So they were different souls. Emily meant something different by that. Magpie needed to get into that room to find the answers to everything. If she could find her way back to it. She met Emily's eyes. "Can you get me back to that room? I tried to open it before, but couldn't."

Emily nodded. "Yes. The door will open when you accept your fate."

Her fate? Was she supposed to die there? She didn't have time to consider that at the moment. She rose and went back to Chase and Donita. "I need to go with Emily to a room she showed me. You should go back to the room with Danny and Jack, you will be safe there."

Chase got up. "No, we are going with you."

Donita rose and stood next to Chase, not appearing so sure. She dropped her head in acceptance. "I'll go with you."

Magpie frowned. What had she gotten them into? Emily

was waiting patiently by a hall entrance out and the three followed her. Well, Magpie did, and the other two followed Magpie. Magpie recognized the halls, but no markings existed from before. They went up a flight of stairs and down a series of hallways until they came to a somewhat generic-looking door. Magpie recognized it as the one before from the handle. Emily pointed at it, then faded away.

Magpie tried the handle, but like before, it didn't budge. She remembered what Emily said about accepting her fate and considered what that meant. She couldn't die before getting the door open, and she couldn't accept her fate without opening the door. So maybe that wasn't her fate. She racked her brain trying to understand the riddle.

What was she supposed to do?

A thought occurred to her, and she silently allowed it to flow through her veins even though she recoiled at the idea. Maybe the haints didn't want to be set free, maybe they wanted something worse. They wanted her forever. Magpie accepted the thought and reached out to grasp the doorknob.

It turned, and the door swung wide open.

CHAPTER 18

J unior skirted through the trees on the ATV, not exactly sure where he was going, but letting his instincts take over. Something he'd pushed down since he was a child surfaced. Back when the visitors came to his room. He told his mother about the couple who sat on the edge of his bed. Barney and Esther. She thought he was making it up and punished him for lying to her. He knew she was only worried about his tall tales... except, they weren't tall tales. They were people who he didn't know weren't there like everyone else until he was older, and he heard ghost stories around the campfire. That's when he came to understand Barney and Esther were ghosts only he could see.

Unlike ghosts in books and on television, they weren't scary at all. They comforted him until he fell asleep. Barney sang songs and Esther told him stories about her childhood. Junior never worried about monsters under his bed or the boogey man because he had Barney and Esther to keep him company. Until he was a preteen and was embarrassed to be different from other kids, so he began to ignore their presence.

Eventually, they respected his desires and went away, never to come around again. Secretly, it broke his heart, but over time, he forgot about his abilities and became a typical teenager.

Until now.

Tyler showing up in his dream cracked open the door a little and Junior could sense he wouldn't be able to stop the visitors from coming through. Junior had Tyler's picture tucked safely in his backpack, and it gave him the sense he wasn't alone. After about an hour, he eased the ATV to a stop and climbed off to relieve himself and stretch. He ate a granola bar and peered through the trees. He didn't know what he was looking for, but knew he'd recognize it when he saw it.

It was calling to him.

After a swig of water and a few stretches, Junior sat back on the ATV and closed his eyes, trying to summon the way. When he opened his eyes, Tyler was standing in front of him. Junior felt like, on some level, he knew Tyler. Recognized him from another time and place. Tyler pointed through the trees, and Junior understood. That was the way to go. He started the ATV and smiled at Tyler, sending a silent thank you.

By dinner time, he was tired of riding and decided to stop for the night. The ATV didn't have a headlight, and he couldn't risk crashing in the dark. He built a small fire and sat close to it, sensing more than the darkness creeping in. Now that the door was open, he couldn't control what came through. He lay next to the fire, then pulled his sleeping bag over him for more than warmth.

It was going to be a long night.

The sounds of gunfire woke Junior a few hours later, and he jerked up, jumping to his feet. He reached to his back for a gun that wasn't there. Had never been there. Junior never fired a gun in his life. He saw shadows running through the trees and flashes of light. Men were yelling and falling as they were gunned down. Junior couldn't comprehend what was happening, but knew it wasn't a dream. A man came straight at him, and Junior braced for the impact. It never came. The man was running at him, then was on the other side of him. It didn't make sense. It was as if the man had passed right through his body. Junior crouched down behind the ATV and watched as all hell broke loose around him.

"You are alright," a gentle, reassuring voice whispered beside him.

Junior whipped around and stared at where the voice was coming from. Tyler was crouched with him, but this time he was dressed in fatigues and a helmet. A military uniform. Junior frowned and glanced down, realizing he was wearing similar garb.

What the fuck was going on?

Then, he realized he *must* be dreaming, even though it didn't feel like it. It was the only thing that made any sense to him. He closed his eyes and willed himself to wake up out of the nightmare.

He let his eyes open a slit and the forest was again quiet. No war, no men, no guns. Junior took a deep breath and collapsed against the ATV. Nothing made sense. If he *was* dreaming, he was doing it on his feet. He scanned around, nothing but eerie darkness greeted him. He knew he wouldn't get any more sleep that night. Junior ate another granola bar and drank water, fighting the exhaustion overtaking him. He waited for the sun to rise and got back on the ATV, grateful for the light.

He continued on his path, aware he would run out of food and gas if he didn't discover what he was looking for soon. More than once, he thought he saw someone standing off in the woods, however, when he focused in on them, they were gone. Even so, he knew it was more than a trick of the light.

Whatever was out there was watching him, good or bad.

Like when he was a child, they wanted him. Barney and Esther kept him safe until he was able to close the others out himself. Barney and Esther weren't with him now, though. He'd made sure of that when he was younger. He was all alone out there.

Even though he'd grabbed the talisman from the earlier checkpoint, he'd left it at the ranger station when he was going through his pack. Just a rock decorated with his blood, but something about it felt more monumental.

He stopped to rest about midday and decided to skip eating. He didn't know how long he'd be out there and couldn't burn through the only food he had. He sipped water and peered up at the sky. He didn't think he could take another night alone in the forest like the one before. He needed to find the other teens as soon as possible. He took slow, intentional breaths and allowed his brain to connect to his deeper senses. The ones that let him know when the visitors were near. The ones that showed him the way.

He understood and got back on the path. Even if the map couldn't tell him where to go, his senses could. A radiating pulse was drawing him in, like a lighthouse that still operated without a beacon, sending intention out over the waves. He knew it wasn't necessarily good, the draw, but he used it to guide him anyway. As it got stronger, he felt a different kind of pull. This one was pure; this one was like him. Magpie's face flashed in his mind, and he caught his breath. She *was* like him, and she was in danger. They all were. Like bugs caught in a web, a predator was coming for them. Maybe had already caught them.

Junior gunned the ATV, no longer needing to wonder where he was going. Like a moth to a flame, he couldn't get out of the way if he wanted to. After a bit, the ATV began to sputter, and Junior knew he was about to be on foot the rest of the way. He didn't relish the idea, however, he was determined to get there in whatever way he could. He was close; he could feel it. Close to what, he didn't know, but it was conscious he was on his way and was delighted to catch another insect in the membrane.

By the time the ATV gave its final push and gave up, Junior felt the vibration so strong, he wondered if it was shaking the ground beneath him. He climbed off and slung his pack over his back. He had the sensation of being pulled toward and pushed away from his target at the same time. As much as something wanted him there, another force was fighting it. He didn't know which was good and which was bad. He put his head down and trudged on. Being in the woods by himself with the pack on his back gave him a sense of familiarity he couldn't quite put his finger on.

After a while, Junior sensed he wasn't by himself out there anymore, and he gazed around. Tyler was walking silently beside him.

Junior smiled. "Hey."

Tyler nodded. "Hey, brother."

Brother. Were they? No, Junior knew they weren't, yet he couldn't deny he knew Tyler somehow. Maybe in a past life. That thought stopped him in his tracks. *Did* they know each other in a past life? "Tyler, who are you? I mean, who are you to me?"

Tyler shook his head, his face filled with sorrow. He pointed at Junior's pack. Junior frowned and shifted his pack forward. He unzipped it and peered in, not understanding. There wasn't anything in there except his supplies and a little food. Tyler frowned and pointed again. This time to the small front pocket. Junior put his hands in the air in confusion, then unzipped the pocket. Tyler's picture was in there.

"Oh, your picture? I took it from the ranger station when I realized you were the same guy from my dream and in the picture. Should I not have? I can put it back when I'm done," Junior offered.

"Look," Tyler said in Junior's head.

Junior pulled the old photo out and held it up. It was a picture of Tyler in his uniform. Like the one from the night before. Tyler pointed again. "Closer."

Junior squinted at the photo. In the background were other soldiers joking around. Tyler was smiling, his head turned slightly like he was laughing at something one of them said. Junior didn't understand what he was supposed to see. Tyler waited. Junior scanned each face and landed on one. A young, slim black man. Not a man, a boy like Tyler. The photo could be a school photo, but it wasn't. It was of boys way too young to be facing what they were, in a war that had nothing to do with them. Junior focused on the boy's face, feeling a connection. A memory.

He dropped the photo.

It was him. It was Junior in another lifetime. A boy on the cusp of manhood, cut down in the prime of his life for another man's war. Why was Tyler a ghost, and he wasn't if that were true? All of a sudden, he understood why Barney and Esther visited him every night. They weren't only visiting a random young boy to comfort him. They were visiting their son. Their son, taken too soon from them. Their flesh and blood from another time. Junior wasn't a ghost because he'd crossed over and come back to the living.

Junior met Tyler's eyes and understood. They were brothers of sorts. Brothers of circumstance and trauma. He picked up the photo off the ground and slipped it into his pocket. Tyler was trapped there because of his guilt of leaving his father, who then committed suicide. Junior needed to help his brother, but he knew it wasn't the time. First, he needed to finish the journey he was on. He needed to find the other teens and rescue them. Tyler was there to help him in his quest. Then, he could create the bridge for Tyler to cross.

As if that thought formed reality, an image appeared in the tree line before him. Rising out of nothing like it had been covered in a cloak of invisibility. Junior stared in awe, knowing for sure it hadn't been there a moment ago. He began to move forward through the brush, his eyes locked on the monstrosity.

A large, decrepit brick building stood where trees once were. It seemed almost alive, lying in wait for its next victim. Its vast windows like eyes boring into his soul. Whatever he was looking for was in there, and he needed to breach it. That much he knew.

What he didn't know was if he would ever make it back out alive.

CHAPTER 19

As the door swung open, the teens took an instinctive step back, expecting the boogeyman to jump out at them. Instead, the door exposed a rather boring and dusty room, partially illuminated by the old windows. Not what Magpie was expecting at all, and she wondered if she'd misunderstood the message. She eased through the opening and peered around. It seemed like an office of some sort. Like an administrative office. On one wall were a series of file cabinets. In the middle of the room were two large desks facing each other.

Chase came behind her and squinted around. "What is this place?"

Magpie shrugged. "I don't know. I guess if people were sent here, they kept information on them, like medical files. It looks like a records room or something."

"So, why are we here, then?" Donita asked, stepped forward into the room, running her finger through the thick layer of dust on one of the desks. "I thought this was, like, a big deal or something."

So did Magpie.

She wandered around the room, opening desk drawers and file cabinets. As suspected, the cabinets were filled with patient records. She rifled through them, not sure what she was looking for. Chase sat at one of the desks and opened the drawers. Staplers, yellowed tape, paper clips. He took out a pen and clicked it a few times. Magpie turned back to the files and took out a handful.

Each file had basic medical and psychiatric records on the past patients. Some had photos included of the patient. What struck her the most was almost all of them had a stamp that read, "DECEASED" across the last page. A few said, "TRANSFERRED" but they could be counted on two hands. For the most part, people were sent there to die. Not a natural death, either, it appeared. Their initial conditions rarely matched their ultimate cause of death. In many cases, their conditions didn't even require hospitalization, and in current times were adapted to and accommodations were made for living a fairly normal life.

Sighing, Magpie sat down on the floor with a stack of files in her lap and flipped through them, searching for why she was brought there to the room. While each case was heartbreaking, it didn't stand out as important to their current situation. Chase moved onto the floor next to her and began flipping through the folders, as well, showing her anything he thought might stand out. After an hour of sorting through patient files, Magpie was ready to give up when a familiar name caught her eye from Chase's stack.

Emily Stanfield.

She motioned to Chase. "Hey, hand me that file."

He slid it over to her, and she placed it in her lap. She opened the dusty cover and was met with a familiar face. A black and white child's picture was clipped to the medical records. Emily. The ghost girl, who was guiding her through the building. Except in the picture, she wasn't a ghost. She was a bright-eyed little girl with a shy smile. The notes stated she had crippling skeletal fluorosis. The doctor noted that there was evidence of excessive fluoride exposure from the family's well, which was the cause of the disease. However, no other family members presented with the condition, and they were unsure of the source of the high amounts of fluoride in the water.

Magpie scanned through the records and was devastated to see at the end a big red stamp indicating Emily had died at the institution. From asphyxiation. Not a side effect of fluorosis. She'd died in the seventies, twenty years before the institution was shut down.

Parents listed as deceased. They'd been healthy when she was admitted as a toddler, then died within months of her death. No cause explained.

Magpie shut the file and closed her eyes. The golden-haired, green-eyed girl now more real than ever. Emily's ghost was still there because she had no home. While the information was a revelation, Magpie didn't feel it was why she'd been called to the building. She'd been called to end it once and for all. To set things right and prevent others from being hurt. Even though the place had been shut down for thirty years, the forces behind it still existed.

"Jesus," Chase whispered, and Magpie opened her eyes, looking at what he was staring at.

It was a picture of an emaciated teen boy, fourteen years old, in another file. He was covered in burns, and his eyes were pleading for help. His condition was listed as cerebral palsy, however, his symptoms in the photo had nothing to do with his disease. They were inflicted by his wards at the institution.

Parents listed as Samual and Margaret Blankenship. Margaret, Magpie's great-grandmother. Reading further into the notes in the file, it appeared the boy, Christopher, had been removed from their home as the state deemed they were too poor to properly care for his condition. A second photo, taken upon admission, showed a much different picture. A nine-year-old boy in a wheelchair with a large smile. Notably, at a healthy weight and no signs of neglect, unlike the picture taken before his death.

Letters from Margaret to the state were in the file, pleading for her son's return to her care. Christopher died at the institution in the late sixties, no cause of death listed, just a red stamp reading, "DECEASED." Margaret had originally visited throughout her son's stay and after he passed to comfort the other children, including Emily. After Emily's death, Margaret had stopped coming for twenty years.

Why she returned in the nineties was a mystery.

Magpie understood how the door was opened. Haints latched onto suffering, and this place was full of it. They'd taken root and stayed long after the humans were gone. It was common in places of trauma. Especially, trauma inflicted by other humans. She wondered why she hadn't seen other ghosts except briefly in the attic. Then it dawned on her, they were hiding from them. Not trusting humans again.

Fair enough.

Chase eyed her. "Did you figure anything out?"

"Sort of. That boy? He was my great-grandmother's son. From the records, it looks like the state removed him from Margaret and her husband, Samual's, care because they were too poor to properly care for him. Or that's what it says, anyway. I doubt that was true, looking at his photos. He died here. I think that's why Margaret kept coming. To protect the other children."

"That's so sad," Donita whispered. "A mother having her child taken away like that, to only die all alone here."

Magpie nodded. She opened back up the file and took out the boy's picture, the one from when he was nine. She realized this made him her family, as well. Margaret also had another child. Magpie's grandfather. The realization of what happened to Christopher made Magpie's heart hurt. She slipped Christopher's picture into her pack, determined to do right by him somehow, even if only by carrying his memory on. Emily, as well.

"So, what do we do now?" Chase asked, waiting for guidance from Magpie.

Magpie glanced at both of them. "We need to burn this place down."

"With us in it?" Donita questioned.

"I honestly don't know. What I do know is that what Margaret started needs to be finished. Everything here, except the ghosts, will fight us on it. They want to be released from here, and if we don't let them out, they will disappear with the building. They need humans to get out."

"Wait, we're humans. If they let us out, wouldn't they be able to go with us?" Chase asked.

It was a legitimate question, and one Magpie wasn't sure she knew the answer to. Unless two different forces were at play. The haints lured them in, and the ghosts weren't letting them go. This didn't make sense because the ghosts could get free, too, if the humans left.

All it took was a living carrier.

Magpie shook her head. "Still trying to figure that out."

"When the building didn't burn and the rescuers came, why didn't the spirits leave with them then?" Donita inquired.

That Magpie knew. "In order to use a human to leave a space, they have to be in a certain state. Humans have different vibrations. The heavier the stress or internal chaos, the stronger the vibration. Spirits can't latch onto high vibrations. The calmer a person is, the more stable their vibrations are and thus easier to attach to."

"Well, I'm sure as fuck stressed out," Chase pointed out.

Magpie laughed in agreement. "Me too. But we are also aware, which makes us more centered. I know it's hard to understand, but the longer we are here, the more we adapt to this reality, and our vibrations drop, making us better targets. Like people who live in war zones. They become used to the high levels of stress so much their bodies find a level of calm to survive. We were vibrating too much when we first got here. Also, when we encountered the entity."

"That's why it stayed in the room?" Donita asked.

"I think there are other forces involved. The thing in that room is trapped there by a spell on the door. The haints couldn't latch onto us at first because of our vibrations. Now, I think the ghosts are trying to protect the outside world, as well, and don't want us to become carriers for the haints."

"Why? After what they went through? Why would they care?" Donita frowned in frustration.

Magpie shrugged. "I think that's why. They knew suffering and don't want others to experience such pain."

"How gracious of them," Chase muttered, not sounding convinced. "Maybe they are using us as bait."

"For what?" Magpie countered. Chase was still struggling with the idea that ghosts were simply part of humans not released, and not scary.

He looked away. "To feed to the haints."

"That's not how it works," Magpie insisted. "Remember, ghosts are just caught souls needing to be released. It's haints we need to be wary of."

Chase shoved the files away and got up. "If ghosts are real, why hasn't my mother come to see me?"

Magpie really didn't want to go down that road, knowing how much he was hurting. She rose and touched his arm, telling him something she knew to be true. "Your mother isn't trapped. She's free."

"Maybe I don't want her to be, so I can see her again." He seemed so defeated, Magpie hurt for him.

"Spirits who are free can sometimes visit. They usually are around, but we don't see them unless we need to," Magpie replied as gently as she could.

Chase's eyes flashed. "I always need her!"

Magpie understood but had no way to make him comprehend how it all worked. "I know you do, Chase. I'm sorry."

Donita glanced at the door. "Should we head back to Jack and Danny before it gets dark? I really don't want to be stuck wandering the halls after the sun goes down."

"Yeah, let's go," Chase said in a huff and headed out of the door into the hall.

Magpie paused at the door, sensing she was still missing something, then followed the other two. After a couple of halls, they weren't sure which way to go, and Magpie searched for the wall markings. While they had been rubbed away, she had pressed hard enough into the wall, so that couldn't be erased. She ran her hands along the walls as they walked, sure they would be able to find their way back. Chase fell behind as the three walked in silence.

Once they hit the stairwell leading to the floor Danny and Jack were on, Magpie turned to tell the others to stay close. The nearer they got to safety, the more the haints would interfere with them getting there. She saw Donita, but Chase was gone.

Thinking he'd fallen behind, she called out. "Chase, come on. We're almost there, and we need to draw in close to each other."

No answer came, and the hair on Magpie's arm rose. They weren't alone. She grabbed Donita's hand and met her eyes. "Don't let go."

They wandered back down the hall, peering into each room for Chase. About halfway down the hall, Magpie's senses went on full alert, and she broke out into a cold sweat. Not only were they not alone, something had taken hold. Another presence was making itself known to her, one she wasn't unfamiliar with. She pushed open a half-closed door and froze in the threshold.

Chase was down on his knees with his hands raised in the air like he was praying to an unseen force. His head was tilted up unnaturally toward the ceiling, and his eyes were rolled back into his skull, showing only the whites. He began laughing maniacally as he shook like he was having a seizure. He rotated his head to face Magpie, and even though his pupils were nowhere to be seen, he looked right into her very soul. Magpie felt the pressure in the room shift as the reality of what was happening washed over her.

"Ah, sweet Magpie. I've been waiting for you. I know you didn't mean to do what you did. You would never hurt me. Now come over here and sit with me, my little bird."

Her grandfather had entered the game.

CHAPTER 20

Magpie froze, seeing Chase, but sensing her grandfather. The problem with their abilities was it interlinked them forever. He wasn't dead as far as she knew, but he'd transposed himself into Chase through what they call spirit strings. Almost like a radio transmission. Chase was the station. Magpie knew there was no point in trying to shake Chase to come to. As with haints, people with abilities and certain spirits could take over a person or even another spirit if they were strong enough. Until her grandfather was ready to let Chase go, he was stuck in limbo. His distress over talking about his mother had made him a prime candidate for being inhabited.

"What the hell?" Donita asked, staring at Chase's twitching form. "What's wrong with him?"

Magpie considered how to explain it to her. They'd all watched horror movies, so she went that route for simplicity. "He's possessed."

"By the haint?"

"Uh, no. Not exactly. More like by my grandpa," Magpie sputtered out.

"Your grandpa? I don't understand. I thought he was in the hospital."

"He is, I think. Kind of. His body is there if he's still alive, but his spirit is here."

"What do we do about it?" Donita asked, her voice saying she didn't want any part of what was happening.

Magpie shrugged in resignation. "I suppose I have to talk to him."

She wandered forward and knelt in front of Chase. Or Chase's body. His blank eyes watched her, and his mouth twisted in a sneer as the words he spoke were long and drawn out in a southern drawl. "That's better, little bird. I knew you would come around. You found the pinnacle, now, didn't you? The door I have been searching for all this time, and here you are. I thank you for bringing me here. After all, it's the least you could do to make up for what you have done."

Magpie was positive she would not help her grandfather in his treacherous intent, however, she needed to play the game to get Chase free. "I'm sorry, Grandpa. I don't know what got into me. I didn't mean it."

She did, and she would do it again.

As if he sensed her words didn't match her intent, Chase's hand shot out and wrapped around her neck like a vise. "You are too strong for your own good, girl. You need to be taken down a notch and remember where you came from and who you are. Family comes first."

While her grandfather was a strong man, Chase was not, so Magpie kicked herself free, moving out of her grandfather's reach. He could hold Chase mentally captive, but controlling his body was another matter. Chase rose to his feet clumsily and began lurching in her direction. It was like a bad zombie movie, but the sight was still terrifying, watching Chase jerking and wavering toward her.

Donita began to scream and scrambled to the doorway. "What the hell is happening to him?"

Just as Chase was over top of Magpie, who was still on the ground, his arms raised to strike, he crumpled to the floor. Magpie grasped his arm and was able to see into her grandpa's soul. What she saw was a fading, frail old man, hanging on to threads of his ability. The effort to come after her had weakened his power. Hopefully, ended his reign of terror. The image dissipated, and she let out a harrowing breath.

Donita was crouched down, covering her face with her hands, hovering in the threshold. She peered through the slits of her fingers and saw Chase lying next to Magpie. "Did you kill him?"

Magpie frowned, then realized how it looked with her clutching onto Chase's arm. "No, he collapsed. My grandpa has left him."

Donita stood up and came over, peering down at Chase. "Is he okay?"

"He will be once he comes back to himself. It's getting dark, we need to move."

They shook Chase, however, he was unresponsive. Magpie sighed and got up, reaching down to lift him under the arms. "Here, help me drag him."

"Won't that slow us down with just the two of us? We will be easy pickings," Donita replied.

"Better than staying here where we aren't protected. He could be out for a while. Like Jack."

They lifted his shoulders and began to move slowly out of the room and down the hall. It was getting too dark to see, and Magpie didn't have free hands to feel the marks she made on the walls. They were in real danger, but she didn't want Donita to know. She could feel the haints closing in on them. While they had been making their presence known even in the light, they were much stronger in the dark.

"Close your eyes," she told Donita.

"What? Why? If I close my eyes, I won't be able to see where we're going."

"I'll lead the way. Trust me, you don't want to see what is about to happen."

Donita closed her eyes and kept moving as they dragged Chase along. Magpie knew what was coming, but it didn't make it any easier. Each room they passed became a view into the hell of what happened at the institution when it was open. The haints were trying to break her.

Magpie kept her eyes down, but she couldn't totally escape the images of patients being tortured in the rooms they passed. In one room, she saw a man strapped to the bed and water poured over his face until he drowned. In another room, a child who couldn't walk was being beaten by the very people sent to protect them.

Magpie knew the child would not survive the beating.

Starving patients, left alone in their own waste to die. Shock treatments and experiments being performed on patients without anesthesia. Children crying for the parents they were taken from. Patients burned and cut as a form of punishment for not being able to do what their bodies were incapable of. It went on and on with each room they passed. Magpie didn't know if Donita could hear the suffering, but she hoped not.

Tears streamed down Magpie's face as she prayed they would find their way to the safe room. She needed help and called on Emily. She peered around but saw no sign of the child. They were on their own. Digging deep into her abilities, Magpie tried to imagine the door of the room, connecting with Danny and Jack.

Danny was frightened and shut down; she sensed that, so he was no help to her. Jack immediately connected back with her, much to Magpie's surprise. He was alive and at least coherent enough to feel her reaching out.

Magpie used that spirit string to find their way back to the room. By the time they got there, both girls were drenched in sweat, their arms shaking. Magpie put her hand out and turned the handle, relieved when it rotated. She eased the door open and peered in. Danny had his back to the wall, his knees drawn to his chest. Jack was lying on the ground, but his eyes were open, facing the door.

"Hey, Magpie, long time no see. Thanks for saving me," he whispered, his voice shaking with the effort.

"Danny, come help us if you can. We have Chase with us. He got possessed but is okay now. He's out cold," Magpie replied, trying to shift Chases's body inside the doorway.

Jack got up weakly, stumbling across the floor toward them. "Not sure how much help I'll be, but let me try. Come on, Danny."

Danny looked unsure but followed. The four dragged Chase through the door and shut it securely behind them. Jack hugged Magpie, his demeanor softer than it was before the entity tried to end him.

"I saw everything that occurred in the room. I couldn't move when the creature had me, but I saw you come for me. I was for sure a goner," he said.

"You could see it?" she asked, surprised.

"Not at first, but when it had me in its grasp, I could see it. That's why I knew I was done for. Until you came. Is that what happened to Chase?"

Magpie shook her head. "Um, no, not exactly. It was my grandpa. He took Chase over."

Jack recoiled, his eyes wide with shock. "He can do that? To any of us?"

"I don't think so. He became weakened by doing that. He was sending me a message that I unknowingly brought him here to this place."

"Damn."

They joined the others and sat in a group. At first, no one

spoke. After a bit, they each took turns telling what happened to them. When Magpie told them what she saw in each room, the others fell silent, absorbing the horrors people not unlike them had endured at the hands of not only the staff but also the other forces that controlled them. Magpie told them about Emily and the boy Christopher, how her great-grandmother tried to stop what was happening.

Exhaustion finally took over, and they took turns throughout the night sitting with Chase, so he didn't wake up confused, as the others slept. Magpie had the last shift with the sunrise and was relieved when Chase began to stir. A revelation had come to her, and she knew what they needed to do. She wasn't strong enough to do it on her own, however. The other teens didn't have her powers, either. She could transfer some to them temporarily, but she wasn't sure it would be enough.

Chase opened his eyes and stared at her as he formed his words. "What happened? I feel like I ran a marathon. My muscles are on fire. The last thing I remember was walking down the hall, and I thought I saw something."

"Something? Like what?"

"I thought I saw you in a room. You were up ahead, so I thought you'd gone in there for some reason. When I got into the room, you weren't there, but I couldn't find the door to get back out. It disappeared like it had never been there in the first place. That was it, I don't remember anything else. Now, I'm here."

"It wasn't me. My grandfather used my likeness to lure you away, so he could take over your body," Magpie answered, half-expecting Chase to freak out.

He didn't. He started to laugh. "Is that why I smell like pipe tobacco and muscle rub?"

Magpie smiled, surprised at his response. "Maybe? Do you remember anything while you were out?"

Chase sat up and ran his hand through his hair. "I had

a cool dream about my mom. She was sitting with me at the beach. We were building a sand castle."

"I like that. I'm glad you got to see her again."

"Ah, it was just a dream. Nice, either way."

Magpie knew better. Chase's mother was protecting him while his spirit was in limbo. She reached out and squeezed his hand. "Good to have you back."

Chase chuckled. "I would rather have woken up in my own bed."

The others began to stir, and Magpie let them wake up before she decided to tell him her revelation. As she sat alone in the night, thinking about what the patients had gone through in the institution, she figured out something she hadn't thought of before. They were still there, hiding in dark spaces from the haints. From the humans. She knew that much.

Why Emily trusted her, she didn't know. But the little girl had openly shown herself to them, without question of their intent. Magpie knew this was the key.

"Hey, can we all gather around? I have an idea that might help us," she asked the others.

They moved slowly but eventually formed a lopsided circle. All eyes were on Magpie.

"As you all now know, I have abilities. We've been wandering lost in this building. Certain entities want us to get out, and certain ones don't, but it's not the way you think. The bad ones want us to get out so they can latch onto us and get out into the world to spread."

"So, who, or I guess, what, is keeping us here?" Danny asked as he drew his knees to his chest.

"The ghosts of the patients. They know if we get out of here, so does evil. They are staying away from us because they've been hurt by humans in the past. Except for Emily. She's helping us."

"Why would she do that?" Jack asked.

"I don't know. Maybe she doesn't understand what the others do. She's little, like six years old. Anyway, I think I figured out what we need to do."

"What?" Chase asked.

"We need to convince the ghosts to join our side to fight back."

CHAPTER 21

I t was as if the building before him was going between worlds, in and out of sight. Junior moved through the thicket toward it, but sometimes when he glanced up, it was like it had only been a mirage. It would be gone, but only for a brief second, a single blink of his eyes, then back again. He chalked it up to exhaustion, thinking his eyes were too tired to keep focused on the structure. By the time he was a few yards away, the building stood as if it had always been there. Crumbling, yet ominous. He glanced around for a sign to explain its existence, but other than a few letters that swung on a wooden board from a rickety nail, absent of the rest of the word, there was nothing.

"Uya," Junior murmured to himself as he sounded out the words. He looked around on the ground for the missing letters, but couldn't find them.

"Uyaga," an answer came from behind him. He turned to see Tyler watching him near the edge of the forest, leaning against a pine tree.

"What does that mean?"

Tyler glanced away. "What they thought it meant, or what it truly means?"

That was an odd question. Junior shrugged. "Both, I guess. Was it the name of this place?"

"It was. Uyaga Institute. The people who built it thought they were naming it after the area," Tyler explained as he walked toward Junior.

"I don't understand. Is that what this area is called?"

"No. See, when settlers came and spoke to the natives, they were told the area was Uyaga. They understood it to be the name the natives called the area."

"The natives? Like Native Americans?"

Tyler tipped his head. "The Cherokee."

Junior nodded in understanding. At least about that part. He still didn't comprehend what Tyler was saying in reference to the name. "So, if they weren't telling the settlers the actual name of the place, what were they saying Uyaga was?"

"A warning," Tyler stated flatly.

This made goosebumps rise on Junior's arms, and he stared up at the rotting building for a moment. He gazed back at Tyler, so many questions in his mind. "A warning about what? What does Uyaga mean, then?"

Tyler shook his head. "Basically, it translates into an ill-intentioned spirit. One that opposes all good."

"So, something that is evil?"

"Sort of. There really isn't a word for evil in their language, but it means a force against what is right."

Junior glanced at the building again and sighed. Now he was even less thrilled to go in there. "Oh. Are the others in there? For sure?"

"They went in there," Tyler assured him. His words were sure, yet Junior sensed something behind them. The others were in the building, but also not exactly, his words seemed to indicate.

"Are you coming in with me?"

Tyler shook his head. "No. Unfortunately, I can't cross the threshold of any structure I hadn't been in before when I was living. I'm sorry."

This made Junior pause, and he turned back to face Tyler. In one lifetime, they were friends, almost brothers. Junior had come back in his current form, but Tyler seemed destined to wander the woods for eternity. It didn't make sense. Why hadn't Tyler come back in human form or at least left the earlier plane?

As if Tyler understood his thoughts, he waved his hand around him. "I suppose I'm not done here. I don't know. I try to let go, but here I am. I was there when you died, you know? We'd gotten trapped on a hill with enemy fire all around us. We were waiting for the Hueys to come in to clear the area, but they didn't come in time. You got hit and bled out before our backup came. I tried to stop the bleeding, but it was too much. You told me to tell your parents you loved them. I never got the chance."

Junior didn't know how to respond to that as the realization of what Tyler was saying dawned on him. "Oh. When did you die, then?"

"About a week later. Stepped on a land mine."

Brothers in war, now standing in a different forest with another battle ahead of them. No, not them. Tyler couldn't go any farther, as he'd said. It was all on Junior now. He shifted his pack and walked up to the door. He was sure it would be locked, however, the handle opened easily. Too easily. His instincts were screaming to run away, but he couldn't leave the others trapped in there.

He turned with a frown to Tyler. "How do you know for sure they ended up here?"

Tyler nodded with a grimace. "I know things. However,

Magpie and I connected, and I led them here when they got lost in the woods, being chased by the bear. They weren't supposed to go inside, though."

"Connected? She saw you?" Junior replied, confused.

"She did. She does."

Somehow, this didn't surprise Junior in the least. Magpie was different; he'd noticed that right off the bat. Not like any thirteen-year-old girl he'd ever met before. He thought back to how she said she tried to kill her grandpa and began to suspect there was more to that than she said.

He chewed his lip as he mulled over his options. "You're sure they're in there? Alive?"

Tyler peered up at the large, dirty windows. "I know they are in there, and Magpie is alive. I'm not connected to the others, so I can't speak to their situation."

Not what Junior wanted to hear, but if Magpie was still alive and she needed him, he had to go inside. The door swung open like the structure was inviting him in. The smell of mustiness and something rotting hit his nose as he stepped forward, and he recoiled. The door suddenly slammed shut as if an invisible hand shoved it hard. Junior jerked back, falling off the crumbling stairs. It was a message. He glanced over to where Tyler had been standing, but he was gone. Whatever existed there, it prevented Tyler from staying and made it clear Junior was in for a fight.

He got to his feet and pushed on. This time, the doorknob fought against him. Junior was big and threw his weight against the dilapidated wooden door, causing it to break into splinters as he pitched forward onto the debris-littered floor. The place was messing with him. Testing him. He needed to get it together if he was going to find the other teens and get out of there alive.

"Hello?" Junior called into the darkness, hoping Magpie would pop into view. He heard his own voice echo back at him and shuddered. The only way in was forward. He took a few tentative steps and was surprised the old, worn floor still held his weight.

He fished a flashlight out of his pack and shone it around the space. It was a large, open room, with two long rooms off either side and a hallway running down from the middle. Doors on each side of the hallway led to flights of stairs, each leading to a different section of the upper building. Junior stood, staring at his three main options, not sure which one to choose.

"Over here," the door on the right seemed to whisper... he knew better than to listen. Everything was going to be a game to try and break him.

He thought he saw a flicker of light down the other end of the hall, a flashlight like his own. He began to move in that direction and stopped. No. Another trick. He went to the other door, the last option, pushing it open. A darkened set of stairs greeted him, and he felt a chill across his neck. In the distance, somewhere deep in the building, he swore he heard a baby crying.

A desperate wail of abandonment.

Knowing the intent, he began to ascend the stairs. Uyaga was going to do anything it could to prevent him from getting to Magpie and the others. There was no baby. Not anymore. Junior cast his eyes down and focused on each step with the flashlight, wishing he had headphones to drown out the sounds he was hearing. Moans, weeping, creepy laughter, whispers in his ears.

As he got to each floor, he paused to see if he could sense the other teens. By the time he got to the top floor, he knew he'd missed something. He went back down a flight and opened the door into the hallway. Shapes crossed between rooms, and the sound of a child giggling behind him made Junior want to run screaming from the building. It meant he must be close. He inched down the hall, opening doors and peering into each room as he went. Shadows played out creepy scenes, but he reminded himself none of it was real. Or not real in the sense it could hurt him.

He hoped.

After opening one particular door, the feeling of a creature scratching inside his skull caused Junior to shake his head violently. It was as if tiny nails were attempting to claw their way through his forehead. His skin began to get prickly like it was being burned with matches. Junior moved faster, attempting to flee the monsters inside him. Dropping his flashlight, Junior stopped and knew he was losing the game. He crouched and scooped up the flashlight. He couldn't afford to leave that behind.

"Breathe," he whispered to himself.

He needed to get it together. If it was trying this hard, he was a threat. Junior rose and gazed back down at where he'd come from. He placed his hand on the wall and felt his way back. Most of the doors were open. One was not. He went and listened outside the door. No sounds came from within. He cast his light on the door and frowned. There were carvings on the door. Symbols. He peered closer and could see that at one time the door had been painted. Nothing else was painted that he'd seen. Or if it had, it was drab colors faded to nothing over time.

This door, however, had leftover flakes of a brighter paint. A bluish-green like the ocean. Strange. He scratched a piece off and stared at it. Why would someone have painted a random door such an out-of-place color? It was almost festive, comforting. The flake of paint seemed to glow bright in his fingers, and a memory surfaced from when he was a child. His grandmother telling him a story when he told her about Barney and Esther. Even though he said he wasn't scared of them, she'd given him a stern warning.

"Junior, you listen to me, child. There are good ones and there are bad ones. The good ones, they can come and go as they please, for the most part. The bad ones, however, they can't cross water. Our people, our ancestors, they knew this. They'd paint their porches and even houses the color of the sea to keep the bad ones away. To prevent them from crossing the threshold. I'm gonna have your daddy paint your room to keep them out."

Junior had cried and begged her not to. Whether or not she ever did tell, or his father thought she was overreacting, his room was never painted the color of water. Bluish-green like the ocean. Bluish-green like the fleck of paint in his hand. Like the paint on the door. Someone was trying to keep the bad ones out of whatever was behind that door. Junior began to bang on the door and call out.

What he didn't know was that the teens inside thought the haints were tricking them and had huddled together into a group against the wall, terrified. Junior tried to force the door open, but it wouldn't budge. On his back, it felt like a thousand wasps were stinging him. He knew he needed to get into that room before he lost his mind. Out of ideas and running out of time, a name trickled through his mind, and he tried one last thing. He yelled with all his might to cross the barrier between the haints and safety. The one thing connecting Magpie and him outside of both being sent to Wilderness Reset.

"Magpie, are you in there? It's me, Junior. I came back for you. Tyler sent me!"

CHAPTER 22

The teens behind the door heard the banging and were clinging onto one another, convinced the haints were finding a way in. Even Magpie was unsure of their safety with the ruckus outside the door. The yelling sounded like Junior, but the haints had a way of making themselves sound like living people. However, they didn't know Junior, she didn't think, so it seemed implausible they would be mimicking him. Then, she heard the words that made her run for the door.

Tyler sent me.

Only she knew about Tyler. She'd been careful not to utter his name and give the spirits a reason to seek him out. If it was indeed Junior outside the door, there was more to him than he'd previously let on. Like her. She grasped the doorknob and pulled with all her might, but the forces in the building didn't want Junior and her coming together. She had her suspicions as to why not.

Magpie leaned against the door and yelled, "Junior, it's

Magpie! I'm trying to open the door from in here, but it won't budge."

Junior heard her from the other side of the door and threw all of his weight against the wooden structure as Magpie yanked from the other side at the same time. The haints may have been determined, but the teens were more so. Danny and Jack came over and joined Magpie in pulling as hard as they could. The knob turned, but the door stood fast. They could hear Junior throwing himself at the other side of the door repeatedly as the thuds shook the door frame.

As the four of them used all of their energy together, the door finally gave way, sending the ones inside the room toppling into a pile on the ground, and Junior stumbling over them. Magpie kicked the door with everything she had once Junior was through. It slammed shut with a bang. Junior caught his footing, and Jack helped Danny and Magpie up. No longer strangers, all the teens came together and hugged tightly.

Magpie smiled at Junior, relieved to see him again. She met his eyes knowingly. "Tyler, huh?"

Junior nodded and glanced around the room. "Yeah. He came to me in a dream at first. Then met up with me in the forest. He helped me find you after he told me you two had connected."

"So... you have abilities?" Magpie asked, already knowing the answer. If Junior was communicating with Tyler, he clearly had some type of abilities.

"I suppose so. I hadn't thought about it for years, but it all came rushing back out there."

"What happened to Brandi and Cara?" Donita questioned. "Is Cara alright?"

Junior shrugged. "Like the day after the day you left, things got bad. I used the flashlight to send signals from the camp. Cara was running a high fever, so Brandi stayed with her, and I waited by the fire. I started seeing weird things in the night, but then the forest rangers showed up. Wilderness Reset sent them to find us. Get this. Craig was rogue. He did something to the other guide before our trip. It sounds like he murdered her."

"Wait, why did he do that?" Chase asked, his face twisted in a frown.

Junior shrugged. "I overheard the ranger saying they were in a relationship. I guess he killed her, then lured us out to the woods."

"What the hell?" Jack whispered. "So they knew something was up and sent someone to rescue us?"

"Sounds like it. They took Cara to the hospital and called my and Brandi's families from the ranger station they brought us to. Brandi left with her father when he arrived," Junior explained.

"Why didn't you go home?" Donita asked.

"I had a dream that you all were in trouble. Tyler, this guy, uh, long story, told me you were trapped. I stole an ATV from the ranger station and came out here. The ATV died a while back, so I walked the rest of the way. With some help from an old friend."

"You know Tyler, don't you? I mean, from before this life," Magpie inquired, not really as a question.

Junior gazed around. "Yeah. Part of that long story. So, what is this place, and why are we here?"

The group sat down and began to tell Junior about their experiences in the building. They told him about the file room and the spectre that had gotten hold of Jack. Magpie told him about Emily and Margaret. Chase, Donita, and Danny took turns telling him the different horrors they'd been exposed to while there. He listened intently without acting surprised or in disbelief.

By the time they got it all out, he was nodding his head repetitively and uttered, "Ah."

Magpie knew he now understood that in order to leave,

they needed to finish what Margaret started. Junior opened his pack and threw them each a stolen granola bar, then pulled out a couple of bottles of water for them to share. After everyone had eaten more than they'd consumed in a while, they rested and talked over their situation and plans of how to get out of the building. Magpie told Junior about her idea of getting the ghosts on their side.

He rolled over onto his side with his head propped on his hand. "How do you think we can do that?"

She chewed her lip. "I don't know. They're hiding from us for sure. We need to get them to trust us, to understand we are trying to finish this and set them free."

"From what you told me, they went through here, that's easier said than done. I can't blame them. I wouldn't trust us," Junior countered.

"I wouldn't, either," Magpie agreed, twisting a strand of hair around her fingertips. "Maybe Emily and Margaret can help convince the others. They trust us."

Junior bobbed his head and sighed, laying his back down. "I'm tired. Let's talk about this in the morning. I feel like I haven't slept in days."

Magpie nodded and let the conversation drop. One thing she now understood was they all needed to stick together. Even though the others, except Junior, didn't have abilities, their presence helped throw the haints off their game. Their game being *divide and conquer*. Jack was back to himself, and although Danny wasn't thrilled with the idea of leaving the room, he'd follow Jack anywhere.

One by one, the group slipped off to sleep until Magpie was the only one awake. She tried closing her eyes, but sleep wouldn't come. She got up and drifted to the window. In the woods below, she could see figures moving throughout the trees. Ghosts caught between worlds. The forest was unsettled in this area. Spirits wandered lost, unable to transcend. It was as if the whole area was under a giant glass dome and nothing could get out. Only in.

One of the figures stopped and glanced up at her, its large, empty eyes seeming to beg for release. Magpie dropped her eyes, knowing she'd get sucked in if she didn't break the connection. Caught souls were hungry, desperate. They could consume anything in their unending need to be anywhere but where they were. This area had some power over them, suspending them in time.

Turning away from the window, Magpie noticed Junior was awake and staring up at the ceiling. She wandered over to where he was resting. She sat down beside him and cleared her throat. "Are you scared?"

Junior kept his eyes averted. "I don't know what the feeling is I have is. You know, Tyler showed me that he and I knew each other. Me in a previous life, him when he was still alive."

"Really? How did you know each other?"

"We were soldiers together. Friends. We both died there, but I was able to go on. He wasn't. It makes me sad to think that I got a whole other life, maybe more, and he's been stuck wandering the forest ever since."

Magpie bobbed her head. "It's not fair. Maybe if we help the ghosts here, we can help him, too."

Junior didn't reply, but she could see his eyes were still open. Eventually, when she looked over, his eyes had closed. She lay down to try and rest. By the time morning came, she remembered something Tyler told her and called the others together.

"Hey. We need to leave this room as a group and stay together no matter what. We have to find a way to physically attach to one another so we don't get separated by the haints. When Margaret tried to burn this place down, she was in the basement. We need to go to the basement."

"Won't we get trapped?" Danny asked.

"I don't think so. There must be a way out of there. First,

though, we need to see if Margaret and Emily can help us connect with the other ghosts. They may be able to protect us as we move down there."

"May?" Donita asked, her eyes large. No one was ready for only possibilities.

Junior chimed in. "If we stick together, we can protect each other, too. We need to do this. It's our only chance of getting out of here."

Somehow, more than a skinny thirteen-year-old girl telling them what they needed to do gave the others a little more courage. Chase got up and fished rope out of his bag. "Magpie and I tied together using this. It's not long enough for all of us, but if we can find a way to attach to each other, even one by one, it should work."

They dug in their packs and gathered a small pile of twine, rope, carabiners, clips, and straps. They fastened together pieces, so with them included, they would form a human chain. Magpie was aware they'd all seen the horrors of the building, but needed them to understand that as they drew closer to their target, the more demented and horrific the attacks would become. The haints couldn't directly hurt them, but they could get enough in their heads to make them hurt themselves.

Or each other.

"Okay, listen up. I'll go in the front, and Junior will go in the back since we both are able to see more than the rest of you. This way, when, not if, the haints come at you, we can make sure you don't get taken away. You're going to see and hear terrible things as we make our way to the basement. Try to keep your eyes down and tune out anything you might encounter, physically or mentally."

"What are we going to encounter?" Chase asked, his voice shaking.

Magpie shook her head. "Whatever scares you the most. Try to remember that no matter how real it seems, it isn't.

Don't unclip, don't leave the group, and don't hurt anyone in the group."

"I'm sorry, what?" Jack questioned, his face twisted in concern. "Why would we hurt each other?"

Junior cleared his throat. "Because you might not know it's one of us. They'll convince you another kid is out to get you, a demon or something. Do you understand? This isn't anything you will see outside of yourself. It will get inside your head."

This caused a visible, collective shiver to pass through the teens as the reality of what they were about to encounter hit them. Seeing something horrible was different than thinking it was real because their brain was telling them it was. They wouldn't be able to differentiate the truth from the images.

Danny rubbed his nose and raised his hand. Magpie suppressed a grin at his politeness and nodded in his direction for him to speak.

Danny glanced around the group, his large, almost black eyes not hiding his worry. "So, is there anything we can do to stop that? Like wear anything or something?"

"Like an amulet?" Magpie asked.

Danny nodded, and the others looked hopeful. Except Junior, who, like her, knew there was nothing but to push through. He met her eyes and gave a brief tip of the head to let her know he had an idea.

"Yeah, there is," Junior offered.

He pulled a wad of twine out of his pack and began biting off sections with his teeth. He wrapped one around each of their left wrists, tying the strand with a knot. As he did so, he chanted what sounded like complete gibberish to Magpie. She questioned what he was doing, but let it proceed as it gave the others something to believe in.

Once he'd done this for everyone, he smiled. "An old spell my granny taught me when I was young. It protects the wearer from harm."

The others glanced at their wrists and seemed to relax with this knowledge. Magpie looked at Junior, and he stared back unblinking, one eyebrow slightly lifted. He had given them all a protection spell to supposedly help keep them safe in the halls from the sinister spirits. A spell, he said, was handed down from his grandmother to him.

One he'd completely made up.

CHAPTER 23

O ne by one, they made their way into the hall, linked by a series of assorted materials and clips. Magpie led the way and paused for all of them to pass through the doorway. Junior shut the door behind him. Once they were situated in a clustered line, Magpie turned to them.

"We need to go back to that room with all of the patients' files."

"Why?" Donita asked, not thrilled with the idea. "We already did that."

"We missed something. I didn't know what I was looking for before."

Chase tipped his head. "You do now?"

No. Magpie shrugged. "Maybe. We know what happened here, and we know what Margaret tried to do. However, we don't know what brought us here or why. I thought it was Margaret, but she doesn't have that power. Something wanted us to find this place. Forced us to. I think everything that happened with Craig was all part of it, as well. Nothing has been random."

Junior coughed lightly. "Yeah, something has been up since day one, if not before. Like with Craig. The rangers said everyone swore he was soft-spoken and kind before he killed the other guide, Katie. Nothing like the guy we met. It was like he was possessed."

This shocked the others, as they let the details of what happened sink in. They'd never been safe since they'd started the hike with Craig. Danny glanced at Jack for clarity, who put his hands in the air in confusion. It was clear they'd been cast onto the path to end up where they were from the beginning.

A line had pulled them in, like fish from a pond.

Magpie frowned. "Remember when Craig was reading off the names the first day?"

"Yeah?" Chase replied.

"Didn't it seem weird to you? Like he knew more than he was letting on, but he also kept messing up."

"I didn't notice anything strange," Jack said. "I mean, he was a dick from the beginning, but most people who do this are. What do you mean exactly?"

Magpie shrugged. "One, he didn't even seem to know I was supposed to be there. Two, he recited the names, barely looking at the paper. Three, he got multiple names wrong."

"I guess so, but maybe he'd memorized our names and just forgot. I mean, he sent the emails and all, telling us where to meet up," Chase countered.

"Isn't that weird, too? *He* sent the emails, not Wilderness Reset. From his personal email," Magpie offered.

They all stood still, considering what that meant, when Junior cleared his throat. "Weird or not, we need to move. I'm getting a strange feeling we aren't alone. My scalp is beginning to tingle."

Magpie felt it too and began to shuffle down the hall.

This time she remembered the way back to the room with the files easier, and had a niggling feeling it was becoming all too familiar. Like she was remembering a place she'd been in a dream. There was no sign of Emily or Margaret, but Magpie trusted her instincts and found the room before too long. She turned the knob and shoved, the hinges of the door creaking loudly as it opened.

As they all moved inside, Magpie peered around, not sure what to look for again. Junior began rifling through the books on a shelf as the others pulled out files. They started flipping through the records without focus.

Danny turned to her. "So, how will we know what we're looking for when we see it?"

Magpie shook her head. "I don't know. This is what we do know so far. This place was open from the fifties until the nineties, when my great-grandmother, Margaret, tried to burn it down. We found out she had a son who was taken away from her due to the time and poverty, or so his file said. He died here, and she came later to try and protect the other patients. Emily being one of them. I think that's why Emily has been helping us all along."

"Which came first? The demon or the egg?" Jack joked dryly as he scanned a file.

"Well, not sure it's demons. There are entities for sure. Haints and the other thing that had you in its grasp. A spectre of some sort. If you're asking if the haints made the people do bad things, I don't think so. Not initially, anyway. I believe it was the other way around. I think the staff were abusing the patients, and their suffering opened the door to allow the dark spirits in. Then, things got worse. Until Margaret got it shut down," Magpie spoke slowly as if to catch a detail she might be missing.

Donita was gazing off, lost in thought. "Okay, so it shut down in the nineties. That's still like around thirty years ago. Why now? Why us?"

Magpie didn't have any of those answers. However, something about her grandfather made her think he'd reopened the wound. That would explain her. Perhaps it pulled Tyler through, where he could communicate with the living, which would explain Junior rediscovering his abilities. The rest of them were likely unintended passengers.

A voice to her left spoke up. "Does it even matter? We're here and need to get the hell out, so let's figure this shit out already," Jack stated.

This seemed to get them into gear, and they each dug into the records, searching for any clue that might help them understand what was happening. One by one, files stacked up without giving them any information as to why they were there. Magpie began sorting through another set of files in one of the lower desk drawers. These seemed to be separated out because those residents were different. None of them appeared to have a disability or mental issue. It was confusing as they seemed to have been sent to the institution as a punishment, rather than as patients.

As Magpie went through each file, she was horrified to learn about the people in them. Adults, teens, even children who were sent away simply because there was something about them that someone wanted to remove. Being outspoken, contradicting authority, disagreeing with family members or churches. None of them survived. A sensation in Magpie told her she was on the right path.

Taking the time to scan each file, she felt her stomach turn with the cruelty she read inside. Even more shocking were the dates. They were the newest files, the oldest starting only four years before the institution was shut down. Something had shifted with the intent of the space over the last few years it was open.

Those files showed a systemic abuse of power. Regular citizens tortured and killed for going against what they were told. For decades, the institution abused the most fragile among them. Then, near the end, they switched gears to create a secret prison to take revenge on anyone who fought back. Notes exposed that the people were marked as mentally ill, so they could be locked away. Even though there was no medical reason to do so. Community leaders' and church clergy's signatures had replaced doctors' signatures.

Magpie now understood what she was supposed to see there. Margaret had experienced her own son dying at the institution and came to stop it from happening again to anyone else. Instead, she'd uncovered a horrible truth. The truth that the place was being used as an illegal and covert dungeon for those who dared question. It was always a prison for the vulnerable population, then they used that power to remove anyone who stood up to the powers that be. Marked as insane and tortured to death for their voices.

Magpie sat down on the floor and flipped through each file. Margaret must have stumbled upon the truth when she came to spend time with the children. Maybe she saw the people locked in there and thought it odd they showed no signs of illness. Perhaps she asked, and they tried to make her leave. Magpie closed her eyes and called to Margaret, needing more answers.

When she opened her eyes, Margaret sat before her. Magpie saw something different in her eyes. A desperation. For some reason, Margaret was unable to speak, but her eyes told a story. One of fear and sadness. Of a mother who'd had her child taken away, only to have him die far from her arms. Of trying to stop others from suffering, then discovered the evil ran beyond the walls of the building. Power-hungry humans willing to torment to keep on top. Haints using the energy created by this torment to make their way through the door and into the world.

Margaret gestured to the files and nodded. She wanted Magpie to keep going, to keep digging. Magpie opened the remaining files, one at a time, scouring the details, even though they hurt her heart. A woman who tried to leave her husband, a mayor. A teenage boy who defied his father when told to kill the family dog for biting the man. A nine-year-old girl who told her preacher she played with fairies in the woods. A teenage girl...

Magpie froze and stared up at Margaret. Margaret held incredible pain in her eyes and pointed back at the file. It was from the year she tried to burn the place down. Magpie glanced back at the file. The girl had been strapped to a bed and given shock treatments for "conspiring with demons". Electrocuted in bed. Magpie couldn't draw her eyes away. There were no pictures, but the description of the girl's death had been written in incredible detail, as if the author had gained great delight from her suffering. The girl's death was marked as a suicide by hanging, even though all the facts showed she was electrocuted to death.

She gently turned the page and let her hand fall to her side. The other teens were going through records, sick looks on their faces. Danny had put a file down and placed his head in his hands. Magpie needed to release them from the horrors laid out before them.

She gazed at them, trying to form words thick in her mouth. "You can stop now."

Junior looked over and his eyes grew wide, knowing she'd found something. He picked up a file from the pile she'd already gone through and opened it. As the realization hit him, he shook his head. "They used this place to kill regular people, too?"

Magpie gulped. "All people are regular people, but yeah. They used this place to get revenge on people not sent here for medical reasons. Locked away to shut them up."

Jack whistled. "That's some messed up shit."

The others remained silent, not believing what they were hearing. They'd already seen the horrors inflicted on people who were deemed "broken" by a small-minded and cruel society, but it went beyond that. There was no end to what those in charge were willing to do to get what they wanted to silence their detractors. That place may have been shut down, but the actions were still in place.

Chase tapped his fingers against his head. "So, is that why we're here? What can we do about it now?"

Magpie met his eyes. "It's not over. That was the first round. We need to stop the next one."

"The next one?" Danny's voice was shaking. "What next one?"

Junior sucked his breath in. "Oh shit. Like Craig, right? It's not contained only in the walls of this place. Uyaga."

"What does that mean?" Donita asked.

"Uyaga. The Native Americans warned the settlers of that, but the white people didn't understand. It's sort of like a bad spirit, but more than that. It's like evil intent. I can't explain it. It used this place and the people's bad actions. It fed it in a way. It's still here, but not just here. What they did to the patients made it stronger, however, it's not only trapped in these walls. Somehow, it got to Craig. Maybe others, right?"

Magpie bobbed her head as she closed the file, slipping a piece of paper from it into her pack. "My grandfather cracked the door open. It wants it to open more, so it lured us in. I think he had something to do with all of this."

"Now what?" Chase asked.

"Now, it's going to try and use us to destroy everything."

CHAPTER 24

The group gathered to leave the file room, and Magpie paused, attempting to determine which way was the basement. Margaret appeared at the end of the hall, holding Emily's hand. They disappeared into the stairwell, and Magpie knew to follow them. She motioned with her head for the others to go with her, and they moved cautiously down the hall. Once they got to the stairs, a shudder ran through the teens simultaneously as if something wicked passed through them all at once.

Magpie took a step down the first stair, sensing the air pushing back on her. This wasn't going to be easy. As if the haints had taken over the very walls of the place, it seemed as if the building was resisting the teens' progress. She pushed forward and felt the tug on the strap connecting her and Chase. She glanced back, and his face was stricken with fear. The mind games had begun. She reached back to him with her hand. He took it, grasping it tightly in his own, comprehending he was being messed with, yet not being able to face it without help.

As the rest came to realize what was happening, they each clasped hands with the person behind them. Except Junior, who was the last of them. He held Donita's hand with one hand and clung to the railing with his other. Magpie did the same, and the awkward caterpillar they made crept down the stairs one step at a time. By the time they got to the next landing, their hands were sweaty, and the exertion of fighting against the forces had worn them out. Magpie knew they couldn't continue at this pace. It was like walking through setting concrete.

Her family embraced their abilities, so they didn't try to stop what came through, instead learned to create a bubble of protection around themselves. Growing up, Magpie had become quite at skilled shutting out the dark spirits and remaining open to the kind ones. Junior was the only other one who had any experience with spirits, so she stopped at the landing and called them together. Everyone seemed relieved for the respite, despite feeling they weren't alone.

"Junior, you said your grandma had spells? Was she familiar with warding off spirits?" Even though Magpie suspected his twine trick was made up, she figured his grandmother might have taught him something.

Junior shrugged. "Not much, to be honest. She was a 'good Christian lady', so anything she told me was more like folklore. Stories, things like that."

"I thought she did spells?" Danny asked. "Christians do spells?"

"Sometimes," Junior replied, and it wasn't completely a lie. In many cultures, the line between Christianity and cultural folklore was hazy.

Magpie's family went to church, but they also practiced the arts, as they referred to their abilities. The two weren't connected necessarily, but both were respected as real and pertinent to life. Magpie didn't like church, but mostly because her abilities allowed her to see right through those who pretended to be holy, all the while harming others. They preached Christianity and danced with the devil.

"Okay, so folklore. What kind?" Magpie asked, not wanting to get off track.

"Well, like the door up there. The one to the room we were staying in with all the symbols? It had at one point been painted a bluish-green. My grandma called it Haint Blue. She said it prevented spirits from crossing the threshold into people's homes. The color is supposed to represent water, and haints can't cross water."

Magpie considered this. She hadn't noticed the paint, but she'd been interested in the symbols and what they meant. "Like what shade of blue?"

Junior's eyes lit up, and he reached into his pocket, withdrawing the small chip of paint. "This color. Can you see it?"

Everyone gathered around and stared at his hand. The chip seemed to almost glow in his palm. Danny reached out to touch it. "It's pretty. That reminds me of my family's lore. My aunt taught me a song when I was little to scare the boogeyman away."

Jack laughed at this, and Danny blushed. Donita eyed Jack with such a sharpness, he dropped his head in shame. "No, sorry. Let's hear it, dude. Anything that helps at this point, right?"

Danny looked unsure, but Junior nodded at him with encouragement. Danny closed his eyes and began singing a rhythmic tune. His voice was rough and cracked at points but the words were haunting.

"I don't know who you are
or where you belong
I don't know your name
but here is my song

This is my space
This is my home
This is my time
Go on now and roam

I am strong and brave
You cannot hurt me
You cannot stay here
I need you to see

Though it may be hard
It is time to leave
I cast you away
This truth I believe

I cast you away now
This truth I believe
This truth I believe."

The song was crude, and Magpie suspected Danny's aunt made it up on the fly, but it had a certain charm to it. She asked him to sing it again, so she could memorize it. The others joined in, making a terrible chorus of teen voices in the throes of puberty. Even so, each time they sang it, it made more sense and came out stronger.

Magpie nodded. "We need to keep singing the song and imagining Haint Blue in our minds. This will hopefully help prevent the spirits from getting into our thoughts. That's their strongest power, twisting our minds. Anything we do to keep our thoughts from being manipulated will help."

The clasped hands again and began the trek down the next flight of stairs, singing badly. It would have been comical if they weren't surrounded by the long fingers of menacing spirits. The singing seemed to be helping, and they made it down the next couple of flights quicker than the first.

By the time they got down to the main level, the teens needed to rest and gathered into a tight-knit group on the floor. Everyone was silent, which was dangerous. Junior began playing I-Spy with the others, even though everything they spied was the same. Hunger pangs were overtaking them, and Magpie knew if they didn't get out soon, they'd begin to weaken due to lack of nourishment.

They were back in the main hall where the stairs came out. However, the door to the outside that was there before was gone. Magpie peered around for anything that appeared like a basement door. Margaret and Emily had disappeared, and Magpie suspected the song they were all singing might have had a double effect.

It likely sent *any* spirits away.

That was the challenge of connecting with spirits. There wasn't a clear way to invite some in but not others. It was actually hard to keep the others out as they latched on to anything moving through the doorway between. All spells and chants were universal, so ghosts often got rebuked by them, as well.

Junior scooted over to Magpie and leaned in. "We need to talk for a minute."

She bobbed her head. "Okay?"

"Listen. I know you said we need to get the ghosts on our side, but how do you think we can do that? What if they won't do it? Do you have a backup plan?"

"I don't know how. I can ask Margaret and Emily to help us, but I'm not sure if that is enough to draw them out. If we can't, I don't think we have the power to burn this place down."

"Why not?"

"Margaret tried, but something stopped her."

"Yeah, but she was only one person trying. We are six," Junior reasoned.

Magpie nodded. "True... but we don't know how many *they* are. The spirits, I mean. It could be infinite."

Junior considered this, then sighed. "We have to make an effort, though, right? What's the worst that could happen?"

Magpie met his eyes, they both knew what the worst that could happen was. There was no guarantee they'd ever get out of that place. Or survive even if they did. Margaret didn't. Whatever happened that day ultimately cost Margaret her life. Her heart gave out.

Magpie glanced at the others. "We can do this. We need to believe that first and foremost. They need to believe it, otherwise, we've already lost the fight. First, though, we need to find the basement."

Junior scanned around, his brows knitted deep in thought. "Well, considering when this place was built, the basement likely also served to preserve food. Like a root cellar. Maybe it's off the kitchen space?"

Magpie hadn't thought about that, but he was right. Everything back then was built for efficiency. If the building had a basement, it was where they also stored back-stocked food. Especially being so remote. It was also where the furnace would be, which was why Margaret tried to burn it down from there. The furnace also may have been fed by coal, making it an easy way to start a fire.

After a bit of rest, Magpie and Junior rose, letting the others know it was time to move on. No one looked thrilled at the prospect but got up, all the same. Magpie tried to remember where she and Chase had seen the kitchen the first time they'd found it. She turned around a couple of times and decided it was off the dining area to the left.

The group reattached their straps and wandered through the long dining hall. A strange light was shining at the far end between the window divider from the eating area to the serving area. Magpie's hair rose on her arms, and she knew getting to the kitchen wouldn't be so easy this time. It was going to be a fight. Something was waiting for them and would try to prevent them from passing through.

As they neared the serving area, it felt like the air had been sucked out of the room. Magpie knew the entity they'd faced before, the one that trapped Jack, was ready for round two and had been released from the room they'd shut it in. Someone had opened the door, likely not knowing what was in the room. It was easy to get confused in the institution and the halls and doors liked to shift their whereabouts.

Magpie felt something come up beside her and glanced up to see Chase walking right beside her. He took her hand with a smile. Jack joined on her other side, clasping her other hand, and the others drew in behind. No matter what, they were facing this together. Their power came from standing together as one.

Chase squeezed her hand and nodded, a nervous smile on his lips. As a unit still holding onto one another, the teens rounded the corner and came face to face with the entity. It seemed even larger to Magpie and she took an involuntary step back out of fear. Jack stepped forward, not letting go of her hand, his eyes fixed on the spot where the entity stood, intending to remove the teens once and for all. Whether or not he could see it, Jack sensed it was there and wasn't going down so easily this time around. Chase joined him, drawing Magpie between them.

Before long, all of the teens were standing in an interconnected row, ready to take the beast on. They clung onto one another and prepared themselves for the fight of their young lives. Everything leading up to this point had only served to make them stronger. More determined. As sinister energy passed through them, one by one they gasped, then set their resolve on what needed to be done.

At that moment, something dawned on Magpie, hearing them gasp and seeing their eyes focused on what at one point only she could see. They *all* could see it now. Not only her.

By standing together and physically connecting to each other, they were able to see to the beyond. Her abilities had spread to each of them because they chose to come together as one. To fight for one another. They'd created a beacon into the other side. As a united group, they were able to confront the entity, and she wasn't alone anymore.

Not this time.

She only hoped it would be enough.

Chapter 25

A foul, acrid stench filled the air, and the teens began to cough uncontrollably. Their eyes watered as the ammonia-like vapors surrounded them. Magpie closed her eyes and attempted to create an aura around them to clear the air, however, the force of the entity was too strong. Its power was far stronger than her own, and it knew it.

She shifted gears and called out. "Be gone with you!"

The entity paused a second, then snickered. It responded in a crackly, almost electronic voice. "Be gone with you, child. You can't take me on."

Magpie knew the way to lose ground was to doubt herself. She met its eyes and smiled. "Wanna bet?"

The others stared at her in disbelief. Then, following her lead, composed themselves. Despite their fear, they fed off each other's energy and became more determined.

Donita wiped tears from her eyes and cleared her throat. "That's my girl."

Magpie laughed and stuck her chin in the air with confidence. The remaining teens began to hurl insults at the entity, which was not what it was expecting. The teens knew their strength came from sticking together.

"You smell like dog shit!" Jack yelled.

Danny nodded and joined in. "Some monster you are, you can't even take a bath!"

"Go back to your corner!" Chase added.

Junior puffed out his chest. "Little, itty, bitty bitch."

This seemed to have the desired effect, as the entity froze in confusion at their lack of terror. They weren't scared; they weren't feeding into its energy. It was enough to throw it off its guard, and Jack darted around it toward the kitchen. Having successfully gotten by the beast, he ran into the kitchen and called back to the others, "Come on!"

They glanced at each other and began to move. However, the entity quickly realized what they were doing and blocked the others from getting through. Magpie quickly considered their options.

"Jack, do you see a door to the basement?" she yelled.

"Yeah, on the far side of the kitchen!" he replied.

The entity, realizing what they were doing, faltered. Go after Jack before he made it to the basement, or hold the rest of them off? Magpie took this chance and called out to Jack. "Get to the basement as fast as you can!"

This made the entity lunge for the kitchen, and Magpie messaged the other teens with her eyes to follow. She went straight for the spectre, then they split into two groups to get around it. Magpie and Chase in one group. Junior, Danny, and Donita in another. The entity now had three targets and didn't know which one to stop. Jack made it to the basement door and yanked it open.

The beast roared and went for Jack, however, the other two groups began to distract it with taunts. It looked like a confused child, moving toward one group, then another. This allowed Jack to make it down the stairs into the basement. Magpie and Chase were close to the door, and she glanced back at Junior. He nodded, understanding.

She needed to get down there.

He began waving his arms and yelling at the top of his lungs. The entity turned on him as Magpie was able to skirt around it and get through the door. Peering back, she saw Junior holding up the tiny paint chip of Haint Blue and the entity stopping in its tracks. Who knew? Junior held it between his fingers as the rest of them sidled along the wall toward the door. The entity didn't move any closer.

Right as they got to the door, the entity lashed out, striking Danny. The boy fell to the floor, unmoving. The others froze, not sure what to do. They couldn't leave him there. If they found a way out, they wouldn't be able to come back for him. If he came to, he might not know where they went or what to do.

Jack was at the bottom of the stairs and hollered up. "Come on! What are you waiting for?"

Magpie glanced at him, her eyes pained. "Jack, it got Danny."

"What do you mean 'got'? Like what it did to me?"

She shook her head at him. Danny wasn't moving. "I don't know. Not like that. It hit him. He's not..."

That was enough for Jack to bolt up the stairs and run into the room. The beast turned on him, but something in Jack's demeanor changed that. It watched him, almost inquisitively. Jack made it to Danny's side and began dragging his friend's body toward the door. Seeing his bravery, Chase joined him, and they made it back to the basement with Danny in tow.

"Is he going to be okay?" Donita whispered.

Junior leaned down and checked Danny's pulse. "I don't know. I don't feel anything."

"Do you even know how to tell?" Jack snapped.

They fell silent for a moment, then Magpie spoke up. "We need to go down to the basement. Bring Danny with us. This isn't over."

They carried the unconscious boy down the rickety stairs and stopped at the bottom. Chase peered up the stairs, eyeing the basement door opening. They'd neglected to shut it in their haste.

"Can it follow us down here?"

"I'm not sure. With the door open, I can't see why it couldn't but it doesn't appear to be. At least, not at the moment. Margaret seemed to think she could burn the building down from here. The only thing that stopped her in the end was the authorities when they arrived," Magpie answered.

"So, a basement that isn't haunted? That's a twist," Donita stated.

This made them chuckle, but only for a brief second while they took in their surroundings. The basement was pitch black, the furnace long since dead. Magpie was hoping to find coals they could ignite to start a fire, however, that was easier said than done. Junior pulled out a flashlight, but the inky blackness absorbed most of the beacon. The light did little more than cast a dull beam a few feet in front of them.

He looked at Magpie for guidance. "What exactly are we searching for?"

"We need to find out how the furnace was run. These old places in this area were heated with coal furnaces for the most part. If we can find any leftover coal, maybe we can light it on fire. Also, look for paper or anything that will burn."

They set Danny's body down along the wall and began feeling around the basement floor with the little bit of light and found discarded paper scraps. When Magpie realized what the scraps were, her heart clenched. Pieces of burned files. Most likely from patients they murdered and wanted to erase any memory of.

That wasn't all they found.

Chase stumbled and fell over a pile of something. When Junior shone his light on it, they all audibly sucked in air. Bones. Human bones, like in the attic. Magpie felt along the walls. They were in another small room. Claustrophobic.

Donita took short, ragged breaths. "Do you think these people died in here?"

Magpie most certainly did. Locked away, out of sight, until their bodies consumed themselves. She didn't answer, not wanting the words to cross her lips. A sudden rush of air hit their necks, and she knew they weren't alone in the dark space anymore... if they ever had been.

Junior was the first to speak. "I guess the basement is haunted after all."

Except something was different this time. Magpie turned and watched as shadows surrounded the teens. She could feel the spirits' deep, aching need, their reaching out to be recognized. To be remembered.

"No, not haunted, but occupied. This is why we didn't see any other ghosts," she answered.

"I don't understand. What are they?" Chase asked.

"These are the ghosts of the people who died here. Who were murdered here," Magpie explained, her eyes focusing on the shifting shapes. "They've been down here all along. I think that's why Emily was hovering by the basement door in the kitchen the first time we passed through there. She was trying to let us know, but maybe couldn't say for fear of letting the haints know."

As if on cue, Emily came forward and took Magpie's hand, surprising even Magpie. Junior cocked his head. "How can she touch you?"

Not only could Emily touch her, all the teens could see her now, as well. The line between here and there had been breached. Magpie looked down at Emily. "Are they stuck down here?"

Emily turned her head toward the ghosts, then nodded.

She pointed at the shadows, which started to form into specific beings. They represented the struggles they had in life, and Magpie understood. No one had released them, so they'd followed Margaret when she tried to set the place on fire. The fire would have set them free. Since then, they'd been caught in the walls of the basement. The ghosts in the attic must have come down to the basement with the teens when they crossed the threshold.

"Margaret was helping them transition, but was stopped from finishing the task. They need us to complete her process and set them free."

"Why was Emily upstairs, then, and not with the others?" Chase asked.

Emily showed Magpie in her mind what happened to her. Magpie squeezed the little girl's hand. "The haints grabbed her before she could cross the door threshold to the basement. They couldn't come down here, and they prevented her from going through the door. She's wandered the halls alone ever since. Margaret must have come back when I showed up."

"Emily's down here now with us, though?"

Magpie nodded and smiled at the child. "She crossed over the door threshold with us when we came through. The other ghosts remaining up there did as well, I believe."

Including Margaret. The old woman stood at the door and gestured for them to follow her. The teens fell in behind her, followed by the ghosts of the patients. Margaret shuffled to a large space with an old furnace at the far end. It was long since inactive, but she brought them there for a reason. If there was any coal left, it would still be around the furnace. The teens began to feel around the floor but found nothing more than dirt and debris from the building slowly decaying. Magpie squinted into the dark and pointed at a shadowy object in the corner.

"Over there. It looks like a large wooden box."

They made their way over and ran their hands along the

box. Its top was open, however, they felt nothing but air when they reached in. No matter how hard they tried, their hands couldn't touch the bottom of the bin.

Jack put his head down into the box. "I'm going in."

"For what?" Donita asked.

"This looks like a coal bin. Maybe there's still some coal left at the bottom."

"Here, let me help you climb in," Junior offered, putting his hands down for Jack to use as a step.

Jack stepped on Junior's cupped hands and threw his long, lanky leg over the side. He paused, a leg braced on either side of the edge of the box, then smiled with a wink. "If I'm not back in ten minutes, call the police." His attempt at levity didn't break the tension, and he shrugged with a lopsided grin. "Well, I tried."

He jumped down into the box, and they heard him scuffling around at the base. All of a sudden, small pieces of coal came flying over the side. Chase darted around, grabbing them before they rolled off into the far corners of the basement, never to be seen again. Jack reappeared, and Junior helped him get back over the edge. Chase gathered the pieces of coal in his shirt and pockets. Magpie hoped it was enough to get a blaze going.

She turned to Junior. "You and Jack go get Danny and bring him close to us. Once this place goes up in flames, we will need to find a way out as quickly as possible before it burns down on top of us."

"Is there a way out from down here?" Jack asked, gazing around.

Magpie considered how they got large amounts of coal down there and knew it couldn't be through the inside stairs. The amount of coal it would take to heat a building of that size would be enormous. There had to be some sort of doorway to bring in loads of coal. She glanced around, then motioned to the only one with a flashlight. "Junior, let me see your light for a minute."

He handed it to her and she pointed it to the floor, waving it back and forth to try and spot what she was hoping was there. Donita tipped her head, peering down where Magpie was searching. "What are you looking for?"

Magpie moved the flashlight around the coal bin and bent down to rub her fingers along the floor. "Here. There are grooves on the floor."

"From what?" Junior asked as he crouched beside her, dragging his fingers through the ruts.

Magpie smiled up at him and waved her hand in the air. "What comes in, must go out."

CHAPTER 26

The teens followed the grooves etched into the floor until it led them to an opening in the outer wall. Not a door, more of a flap designed to slide coal bins through. They tried pushing on it, but it wouldn't budge. Junior threw all of his weight at the seemingly decrepit wooden divider to the outside world, however, it was like it was made of concrete. It didn't make any sense. Then again, not much had so far.

"What do we do?" Chase asked, rubbing his head in confusion. "I don't understand why it won't move."

Magpie sighed. "It's not the wood stopping us. I don't think this will open unless we close the other door."

"The other door?" Donita peered around as if there was a door she'd missed somewhere in the basement.

"Not that kind of door," Junior replied. "Like a portal door. Whatever let the haints through."

"Oh." Donita deflated. "How do we do that?"

"By burning the place down," Jack interjected.

"Doesn't that seem risky to hope that by burning this place down, we will miraculously get out through this flap thing?" Chase replied, not convinced of the plan.

Magpie nodded. "It is, but do you have any other ideas? We are running out of options."

They all fell silent. No one did. A cold gust of air hit their necks, and Magpie gazed around. It was coming from inside the basement. Something sinister had latched onto them when they crossed the threshold and was making its presence known for the first time. She stood up and walked toward the source, feeling a pressure building inside her head. The sound of suffering clawed at her skull, so she closed her eyes, trying to shut it out. It wasn't working. The haints had joined together to bring them down.

The other teens sensed the shift and soon were being terrorized, as well. Chase grasped the sides of his head and groaned. Donita seemed frozen in place, her eyes large and terrified. Jack fell to his knees, then vomited. Even Junior, who held the sliver of Haint Blue paint, was not immune. He began to shake, his eyes rolling back in his head. Magpie knew they needed help to continue on.

"I call on you, spirits of this place. You, who were ignored and tortured, suffering needlessly. I ask for you to help us end this once and for all. We need you. You need you. Please show yourselves to us, so we can help."

The basement remained silent. She could feel their presence, but they were still scared. Especially with the dark presence now showing itself in the basement. Their safety had been compromised. The sensation of pain increased in the teens' bodies, and they fell one by one to the floor. Magpie tried to hold out, but the pain became too intense to bear, even for her. It was the pain of all the suffering combined. The others were twitching and crying out as if their flesh was being seared from their skin. Magpie closed her eyes and prayed for a quick end to the pain.

The sound of chanting forced her to open her eyes, and she saw Margaret standing in the middle of the room, her arms outstretched as if she were welcoming others to her. Her white, loose gown seemed to move as if blown by the wind, and she was repeating over and over a call to arms.

"My children, be not afraid. These young ones have come to set you free, but they need your assistance. Come, my babies. Come, my loves. It is time to rise together and destroy what has harmed you. To finish what I started so many decades ago. They can't do it alone; they need you. Please stand with them to end this."

Emily appeared at her knees and raised her arms in the air with a giggle. One by one, other spirits appeared in their human forms and encircled Margaret, their eyes shining in her presence. In her living years, she had come to protect them, to set them free. They trusted her. Magpie felt the pain ease and knew the haints were turning to face the ghosts. She stumbled to her feet and cast a protective aura over the other teens.

As the agony subsided, they helped one another to their feet and stared at the scene before them. At least fifty or sixty ghosts had gathered and were standing with Margaret in a battle line. The haints also took shape and went at the spirits. They were aiming for Margaret, knowing she was the ghosts' source of strength, and the teens knew they couldn't let that happen.

Jack winked at Magpie and cleared his throat. "Look at you tiny, ugly demons. I bet I could destroy you with one hand tied behind my back."

One of the haints spun and roared at him. Donita stepped back and glared at Jack with rage. "Shut the hell up! You'll make them come at us."

Jack shrugged. "I thought you were a bad ass. Let's see some of that brawl bitch now."

Junior laughed, and Donita turned on him. "This isn't funny. They could kill us all!"

Jack focused his attention back on the haints. "Come and get me," he taunted.

Magpie knew what he was doing. He was trying to trick them to weaken their powers. At current count, there were six haints; with the ghosts and the teens, the haints were outnumbered by scores. The haints could only win by intimidation, so the teens couldn't act intimidated. They needed to believe in their own powers.

Jack flipped them off with both hands and snickered. "What? Too scared?"

Chase had always been the reasonable one, however, he joined in and mooned the haints, pulling down his pants with one hand. Magpie couldn't suppress a giggle at their tactics. The haints, however, were not amused and shifted their focus back to the teens. Margaret caught Magpie's eye and tipped her head toward the furnace. She needed to separate from the other teens to set the fire.

Chase still had the coal clutched in his shirt, and Magpie needed to get it. He was pulling up his pants with his free hand and clutching the coal in his shirt with the other. Magpie ran up to him as the haints moved around them.

"Give me the coal," she whispered.

He dropped his eyes to hers and nodded, understanding. She tucked the coal pieces into wherever she could—pockets, down her pants, curled in her shirt, then stepped away. The haints were closing in on them; they were running out of time. Donita, seeing Magpie needed to get away, did something unexpected. She stuck her chin in the air, her deep brown eyes blazing with rage.

"You aren't shit, you wispy-ass gremlins! You can't hurt us. You're nothing more than a story told to children to keep them from straying too far from home. Go back to your hole in the ground!" Her voice was strong and sure, even though her shoulders shook.

The haints had it with the teens and combined to get into

their heads and drive them mad. They encircled the kids in a cloud of black smoke, however, Magpie had been able to slip free as Donita distracted them. The teens began to scream, and Magpie felt their torment. She wanted to help, but a look from Margaret let her know she had a job to do to set them all free for good.

She ran to where the furnace was. Margaret was right beside her, as was Emily. Magpie glanced back at her friends, expecting to see the worst when she saw ghosts creating a glowing wall between the teens and the haints. No longer scared and hiding, they were willing to fight back. The haints went at them, driving many to the ground, but the line held.

For now.

Magpie piled the paper and coal, searching around for a way to light it, when something sailed through the air at her. She instinctively reached out and caught it, looking to see where it came from. Jack was grinning and pretending like he was smoking a cigarette. Magpie glanced at her hand and saw it was a lighter. Jack had smuggled in a lighter to smoke cigarettes on their excursion with Wilderness Reset. Of course, he had. Their eyes locked, and she grinned at him in appreciation.

They weren't so different after all.

Crouching down, Magpie lit the paper and blew on it to catch a flame. The coals were old and didn't want to start, but she kept giving them gentle air to keep the tiny flame alight. This caught the attention of the haints, who attempted to come over to her, but the wall of ghosts blocked their way. The teens whooped and hollered as the flame grew. The first coal caught, as Magpie held her breath.

This had to work.

One of the haints broke free and darted toward Magpie and the small fire. Margaret stood with her arms stretched out before her in a protective aura, and it faltered. The coal finally caught, and the fire grew. The floor was concrete, so

Magpie knew she had to spread the coals to the walls to catch the actual building on fire. She peered around for something to move them, when she felt someone beside her.

Chase smiled. "Let's do this."

The teens used random items from around the basement, such as rods and tools they found, to move the coals to various piles against the walls. Some fizzled out, but others began to catch. Much of the walls were brick, however, the beams and supports were wood and went up quickly.

As the basement lit up around them, they clapped and danced around in amazement. They'd done it. Even the haints were stunned and frozen into silence. Magpie met Junior's eyes and gestured toward the wooden flap, praying it would open now.

He bobbed his head and got the others' attention. "We gotta go before the whole place comes down on top of us."

They ran for the flap, hoping they could get through it. After a few kicks and shoves, the wood began to splinter. Magpie noticed the haints' eyes light up, and she realized they were going to try and latch onto the teens to get out into the world.

She couldn't let that happen.

"You go first, I have to hold them off. You'll need to invite the spirits of the deceased with you to set them free. I'll follow behind," she ordered. She ran over and slipped Junior the piece of paper from one of the files. "Please hold onto this paper so it doesn't get burned. Put it into your backpack quickly."

He did as he was told and watched her. They all appeared unsure about leaving without her, but the flames and falling beams left them no choice. Each teen turned and invited the ghosts to latch onto them as they moved toward the flap. As each one left, they turned to see Magpie, who was now standing with Margaret, creating a prism of light that held the haints at bay.

212

"Way to go, Magpie!" Chase yelled as he darted out with dozens of ghosts around him.

"You're one bad bitch! Respect!" Donita hollered back, right before she slipped out into the night, ghosts clinging to her everywhere.

"See you on the other side!" Junior said, smiling at her with pride. He opened his arms to a slew of ghosts and gathered them close as he stumbled out into the woods.

Jack had Danny slung over his shoulder, and Magpie frowned. She motioned for him to come over to her before he crept out through the opening. He did, and she and Margaret each placed a hand on Danny, sending some of the light into his body.

Magpie touched Jack's cheek, appreciating the connection they'd formed. "Go on, now."

Jack leaned down and kissed her forehead, then went out into the night with Danny and Emily, the last of the ghosts except Margaret. Margaret was with Magpie until the end. They needed to make sure no haints got out into the forest. Magpie scooted back toward the opening and could see the others standing outside, waving for her to come with them. The ghosts were drifting off into the forest, finally free of their torment and years of imprisonment.

The teens had done it; they'd released the ghosts. The haints fizzled into nothingness as the building lost its control and power, shutting the portal door. Magpie could hear the teens calling out to her.

She waved back at her friends and smiled as the building collapsed down around her.

CHAPTER 27

"**M**agpie!" Chase screamed as he and Jack tried to race back toward the opening to rescue her. The heat coming off the building and the falling debris stopped them in their tracks.

The flap into the institution was obliterated by the crumbling structure as bricks and part of the chimney crashed to the ground. The teens desperately scanned around for a way back in, but as hard as the building had been to get out of, it was impossible to reenter. Danny, who'd until that point been unconscious, began to stir and gazed around in confusion at the engulfed structure.

"What happened? Are we out?" he croaked painfully, making an effort to sit up.

Jack nodded, his eyes still fixed on where they'd last seen a glimpse of the girl who'd led the way and saved them all. "Not all of us."

Danny followed his gaze, then glanced around at the

other kids, taking a mental tally of who was out there. "Where is Magpie?"

No one needed to speak as her absence was monumental. Donita began to cry into her hands, showing a softer side they'd yet to see from her. Chase fell to his knees and cupped his head in his hands in distress. Jack tried again to approach the building, but the wall of flames made it a non-issue. Whatever was in there was nothing more than bone and ash.

The teens watched the structure disappear into the night as the sun rose in the sky. They couldn't move and didn't speak. There was nothing left to say. As the brick and wood became a smoldering pile of rubble, the reality of what happened came over them. Junior had been oddly quiet, and the others were lost without their guide. Not Craig. Magpie.

She'd been their leader all along.

Finally, Junior got up and peered around, his shoulders slumped. "We need to get moving."

"How can you say that?" Donita asked. "You want us to just leave her here?"

"She isn't here anymore," Chase muttered, joining Junior in standing. "We fucking let her burn."

"No." The response came from Jack, who'd danced on the other side and come back. "She never planned to come out. I see that now. She was saving us, so that meant she had to stay behind to finish it."

None of them could disagree. Magpie had met their eyes with a smile and let the building take her. She'd set them free. Set them *all* free. The ghosts had wandered off into the forest, and the teens could still hear their whispers in the boughs of the trees. They, too, were finding their way after decades of hide and seek. It made the forest echo with a cacophony that had never been heard by human ears before. It was disturbing, yet soothing.

Jack helped Danny to his feet and reached out for Donita. Surprisingly, she took his hand as a wobbly smile touched her lips. They all started as resistant strangers, and now were more than family. Eight had become five. Chase glanced at the others with a frown.

"Do you think she's trapped in there? Not her, like she was. Like her spirit?"

Junior stared at the rapidly disappearing building, then out to the forest. "I don't think she ever was."

For some reason, that made sense to all of them, though they couldn't explain the reasoning. It was as if Magpie could have walked out of the door at any point, but chose to stay with them to make sure they made it out alive. Maybe that was her abilities, or her heart, they couldn't say.

Jack called out to the trees. "Magpie, you are one of us. Forever."

They began a slow trudge toward what used to be the road, now simply different vegetation. Even so, the path now seemed more visible, as if the institution going up in flames cleared the way for them. They didn't know where they were going, but they couldn't stay there.

Junior paused and faced the group for a moment. "We need to dry brush ourselves."

"What?" Danny asked, confused.

Junior began using his hands to act like he was brushing dirt off his body in broad strokes. "Like this. We need to make sure none of the spirits are still latched onto us. So they don't follow us home."

The others began doing the same. All except Jack. He shook his head, tears filling his eyes. "Just in case."

They understood what he meant. One of them needed to make sure Magpie had a way back. Junior nodded with appreciation. Jack had been the hardest on Magpie in the beginning, now he was the most connected to her. They finished the dry brushing and began walking again in silence. After only about thirty minutes, they heard the sound of a vehicle and froze in their tracks.

It couldn't be.

A ranger vehicle came bouncing over the rough terrain and slid to a halt when the driver saw the teens. The ranger from before at the station jumped out, his eyes wide. "There you are! We have been searching high and low for you! Man, you kids have had a lot of people worried."

"You found us," Donita replied flatly.

They shuffled to the vehicle as the ranger eyed Junior. "I guess I can't be mad you stole my ATV since you found the others, but, son, that was a stupid thing to do. You could've gotten yourself lost, or killed."

He had no idea. Junior hung his head. "I'm sorry, I couldn't leave them out there, sir. They are my friends, they needed me. I needed them."

"Where have you all been this whole time?" the ranger asked.

"Whole time? How long were we gone?" Donita asked.

"You were gone for almost two weeks. We had about given up, but we thought we saw smoke and followed it. Did you see anything burning out here?"

They glanced at each other sheepishly when Chase spoke up. "Damn right we did. That monstrous building."

The irony that he ended up on that journey in the first place for trying to burn down a building wasn't lost on the others, and they began to laugh. The ranger frowned, not getting what was funny. He shook his head, chalking it up to exhaustion and delirium.

He shrugged and opened the passenger door. "What building? We can't find the source of the smoke," he replied, rubbing his head in confusion.

"Uyaga Institution," Junior answered, pointing in the direction they'd just come from.

"I heard about that place, but always thought it was an urban legend thing. Never saw it for myself. But if it's true what the stories say happened there, I say good riddance." The ranger got on the radio and called the other rescuers to let them know he had the teens and which direction they said the building was in. "Let's get you kids back to safety. I'm sure your families are desperate to see you."

They climbed into the vehicle, having to practically sit on one another to fit in. Junior got in the front with the ranger, while the others dogpiled into the back seat. The ranger paused before he started the vehicle. "I guess I should do a roll call."

The teens glanced at each other, trying to think how to explain what happened to Magpie. They obviously couldn't tell the ranger about the ghosts, haints, and a building that wouldn't let them out.

The ranger pulled out a notepad and squinted down at it. "I'll just say first names, if that's alright. Danny, Chase, Junior, Donita, and Jack. That right?"

They all nodded and gave each other furtive glances. Chase leaned forward. "Is that all?"

The ranger looked back at the notes and cocked his head. "Oh, well, I mean, Brandi and Cara, too, but they were rescued earlier. Cara's doing well, I might add. Healing up nicely."

"Magpie?" Donita asked.

"The bird?" the ranger replied, clearly befuddled.

"No, a girl. Magpie Abernathy?" Danny added.

"Uh, no. I have the roster here, that's all that's listed. I don't know if you are aware, but this trip wasn't even sup- posed to happen. The guide, Craig, killed the other guide. I guess they were dating, and one night, after the last group of teens went home, he lost his mind and murdered her. Wilder- ness Reset tried to cancel your group when they couldn't get a hold of Katie, but he took you out anyway. He used your emails and sent an itinerary, after telling Wilderness Reset he'd cancelled the trip. They were shocked by this behavior as he'd been a guide with them for years. Never had any issues before this. They said this was completely out of character for him. Had always been a nice guy."

Junior remained silent, remembering the night he saw Craig's spirit watching him from the tree line. Coming closer and closer. Craig may have once been a nice guy, but something had taken him over. Something that wanted to get to all of them. To stop Magpie. From the moment the excursion had been planned, another plan had been set in motion. This made Junior think of Magpie's grandfather, and he wondered if he ended up living.

"Um, sir?"

"Yeah, son?"

"You know these parts, the people around here pretty well. Do you know the name Abernathy?" Junior asked.

"Sure, they've been around for years. Was that the name you were asking about earlier?"

Junior nodded. "What do you know about them? Are they good people?"

The ranger grimaced and met Junior's eyes. "I can't speak for all of them, but that old man, the grandfather, he was a terrible person. People still talk about his way of being. Racist, cruel, mean as all get out, if you know what I mean. I think the world breathed easier when he died."

"He died?" Chase asked, not hiding his surprise. "Like in the last few days?"

The ranger frowned, not understanding the question. "Maybe we aren't talking about the same person, then. I'm talking about the patriarch of the family. Margaret's son. Her other boy died mysteriously as a teen; he was disabled or something. Anyway, her other boy, the man I'm talking about, was demented as long as anyone knew him. Into the occult or some such nonsense, people around here said."

"Yeah, that's who we're talking about," Chase explained. "We knew his granddaughter."

The ranger laughed and shook his head. "Are you trying to pull one over on me?"

The teens stared at each other in confusion. What was he talking about?

Jack spoke up. "How did the old man die?"

The ranger rubbed his chin with one hand as he guided the Jeep with the other. "Story says the family had the sight. You know what that means? They could communicate with the spirit world and the such. He used it for evil, supposedly. Wanted to commune with the devil or some other unholy garbage. One night, as he was doing a ceremony to bring forth demons to do his bidding, his granddaughter stabbed him. He died later in the hospital."

Junior played along. "What happened to her?"

"I think the story goes she was committed to a mental hospital since she was just a girl, like twelve or thirteen. After that, I don't know."

They fell silent, trying to understand. Jack shook his head. "No, she was with us. On the trip. We were trapped in the building, and she helped get us out."

The ranger laughed. "I think you inhaled too much smoke. Son, the situation I'm talking about happened in the nineties, going on thirty years ago."

Junior felt an odd tug at his pack and remembered the paper Magpie had given him to make sure it didn't burn. He drew it out of his backpack and unfolded it slowly, almost afraid of what it contained. It was from one of the files about the patients. His eyes grazed the document until it fell upon words that made his blood run cold.

"Magpie Abernathy, age thirteen. Deceased. Admitted for paranoid delusions and violent tendencies. Found hanging, strangled by her bedsheet. Ruled suicide. 1995."

CHAPTER 28

The teens handed the paper around to one another, attempting to understand what just happened. Magpie had been real. Flesh and blood. They were sure of it. They'd hugged her, held her hand, fought alongside her. There was no way they'd made that up. However, plain as day, the paper told a very different story of the girl they knew. She *had* stabbed her grandpa, that was true... decades prior.

It didn't make sense.

If she'd died then, how was she there with them? They fell silent, each letting their minds run over the possibilities. Craig didn't have her on his list, they remembered that. He also had Danny's name wrong and didn't even have a last name for Junior, so that alone didn't raise any alarms. Except no one was looking for Magpie. The ranger said she didn't exist.

Chase rubbed his head and handed the paper back to Junior. "So, what does this mean? We're all nuts, or Magpie was a ghost?"

"She was a ghost," Jack answered matter-of-factly. "Now it all makes perfect sense if you think about it. She knew things we didn't from the beginning. She was able to take on the haints. She always seemed one step ahead."

"Yeah, but she could have done that in life, as well. She told us that," Danny pointed out, his dark eyes darting between them. "She had special powers."

"Abilities, not powers. She wasn't a superhero, Danny," Donita said in a tired but admonishing way.

Junior laughed. "She sure seemed like one at the end."

The end.

They'd all watched her disappear beneath a waterfall of fire and ash. If she'd been alive, she wasn't now. However, there was no death to report, no need to send in search and rescue. Where was she now?

"Do you, uh, do you think she was set free like the others?" Chase asked.

"I don't think she was ever trapped," Jack answered. "I think she was always there for us. For them."

"But wait, didn't the place, the haints, want her pow-, I mean abilities. Didn't she say her grandpa wanted to use them to open the, like, doorway?" Danny questioned. "Why would it want us? If she could walk out, why didn't she?"

None of them knew the answers, however, they did know she stood with them to get them out alive. She was one of them, regardless of who she was or how she joined them. They didn't have much more time together before they all went their separate ways.

The ranger came in and nodded at the cluster of teens. "I have called everyone's guardians. The police are also on their way... again. They're getting real familiar with you lot. They will have some questions about what happened when you got lost in the woods. Hell, I think we all do. There are sodas and snacks in that cooler over there, feel free to help yourself. I'm writing up my report now and will let you know when people start to arrive."

"Sir, did you ever find the building? Was anyone still there, by chance?" Chase asked, hoping against hope they found Magpie alive, even though he knew better.

The ranger frowned and shook his head with a sigh. "Look, I don't know what you think you saw. We scoured that area high and low and didn't find anything. There is a tale of the building from way back in the day, but we couldn't find it. I assume it eventually got picked apart by locals, and the rest became part of the earth. However, we couldn't find any sign of it. The police are going to go back out with some infrared tools to see if they can find the source of the smoke, but there is no building."

They couldn't convince him otherwise, and like Magpie, they began to question what was real and what wasn't. They knew what happened to them was real, however, now they weren't sure exactly how it all came about. Over the next few hours, the teens ate and slept, something they hadn't been able to really do for days. They also talked about what they would say to police to keep their stories the same. The truth sounded crazy, and they needed to agree on a lie. They were getting pretty good at that, considering.

They conspired to tell the police they were simply lost in the woods and came across a building to seek shelter in. It accidentally burned, and they ended up back in the woods when the ranger found them. Keep it simple and close to the truth without elaborating. They all decided mentioning Magpie was not for the best.

The police came as families began arriving and spoke to each teen alone. They all stuck to the script. It seemed to satisfy the authorities, who were more concerned with Craig murdering Katie and later falling off a cliff. At least the teens were back safe, and they could put that to bed.

Before they were separated again, the group exchanged contact numbers and promised to stay in touch with each other. By the time they were leaving, they'd followed one another on social media and texted one word between them. Uyaga. They needed to remember. Then, they formed a group chat called Magpie.

It wasn't over.

The police searched the woods for the burned building or any type of remnants with specialized equipment, but also came up empty-handed. If it had been there, it somehow managed to slip back into the forest unseen. Not even a pile of rubble. It simply vanished into nothing. They asked the kids if they were sure of what they saw, but all of them shrugged and said they were pretty exhausted at the time and hallucinating from lack of food and water.

The teens knew better.

Once, there had been an institution where people were sent away. Out of sight, out of mind. Some because their bodies worked differently, some because their minds worked differently. It had been constructed on tainted land and run by cruel people. Maybe they didn't start out that way, but soon their minds turned, and they tortured the residents. Murdered the residents. This suffering allowed dark spirits to take hold.

Dark spirits Magpie's grandpa called to himself to gain power. She stopped him, but he stopped her. She was locked away and never came out alive. Margaret, having lost a child to that space prior, had gone to try and save her and the others, but was too late.

So, she tried to burn it to the ground.

What none of them knew was that no one walked out of there alive for long that day. The remaining residents and staff died within days from injuries, neglect, and suicide. Margaret's heart gave out on the way to the hospital. The paramedics, Judy and Gary, died in a freak accident a week later, veering off to avoid an old man in the road.

An old man who wasn't there.

Any firefighters or police on site that day were killed in the line of duty within months. Even nurses and doctors, who cared for the patients rescued, had strange circumstances befall them. Before long, no one remembered the true stories of Uyaga. It became an urban legend.

No person was left to tell the tale of the horrors that unfolded in that place. So, it lay in wait for a group of misguided youth to come wake it up again. But why? None of it was an accident. What the teens didn't know in their confused, puberty state was that *each* of them had abilities. Junior could see the dead. Jack could trick spirits. Chase created a bridge between worlds even he didn't know about. Danny was a barrier, a protector. Donita could see into the past.

Even Brandi had a secret she didn't tell anyone. She'd heard voices since she was a little girl; she called them angels. They warned her about people's intentions. She tried to send them away by drawing herself close to those very same people she was warned about.

Predators and users.

Cara was the most dangerous of all to Uyaga, which is why it had Craig poison her. What appeared as appendicitis was her body reacting to the poison, shutting the organ down. Cara's ancestors knew Uyaga well and had kept it contained through rituals. She'd chalked it up to folklore, but her grandmother often taught her chants and songs to keep the dark spirits at bay. She was who'd unintentionally called to Magpie, her soul knowing what her mind didn't. They were in danger. They needed her help.

Something had brought the teens together, but for what purpose? To end Uyaga once and for all, or to use their abilities to open the doorway wider? Something had also clearly taken over Craig's mind and caused him to not only kill the woman he loved, but to try and take down each of his wards with Wilderness Reset. He was no longer Craig, rather a conduit for an ill-intentioned entity.

The teens embraced as they left to go their separate directions. They'd won this round, but something told them the game was far from done. The building was gone, the spirits cast back to where they'd come from. However, like good and evil, it always remained. They couldn't silence the forest; they wouldn't stop the energy lying in wait for the next opportunity to release into the world. One day, probably without intent, someone would crack open that door again and release the monsters.

Until then, life would go on.

Junior was the last to go, his aunt driving a far distance. He stood on the edge of the clearing, staring off into the ever-darkening trees. A familiar figure stepped out from behind a thick tree trunk and waved at him. Tyler. Junior moved toward him, and for a moment between two worlds, the friends embraced.

Junior stepped back and smiled. "I wasn't sure I'd see you again."

Tyler nodded, his eyes heavy with sadness. "You always know where to find me."

"Does that mean you're still stuck here?"

Tyler glanced around. "Seems so."

Junior frowned as headlights made their way up the thin trail. "I think my aunt is here to take me home. I don't want to leave you, though."

Tyler smiled and shook his head. "You never have."

The ranger came out to greet Junior's aunt and motioned Junior to come over. "Hey, son. You're ride is here for you. You ready to go?"

Junior paused, stuck in two realities. Tyler helped Junior in a previous life to cross over, Junior wanted to be able to do something for Tyler. He glanced at his aunt's car and thought about Barney and Esther.

And Magpie.

He tipped his head at Tyler. "Did you know?"

Tyler appeared confused and shook his head. "I'm sorry, did I know what?"

"That she was a ghost?"

Tyler bobbed his head. "I did. However, she didn't. She thought she was just another teen."

Junior considered this and dug his sneaker toe in the dirt. "She *was* just another teen. Looking for acceptance, trying to do what was right, being misunderstood. She was one of us. She *is* one of us."

Junior could hear his aunt calling to him and turned in her direction. She was chatting with the ranger and paused to wave him over. Junior felt a tug at his heart and faced Tyler. "You are my brother. My friend. Your time here is over, I believe that. You can't spend eternity wandering these woods. Listening to the sounds of lost souls. You deserve to have a family, a place to call home."

"I lost that when my father died and our home was destroyed. I don't have a home anymore, and I'm trapped here until my soul is at rest. I'm not sure when, or if, that will happen."

"I don't know about the second part, but I can do something about the first part," Junior offered.

"What part?" Tyler responded, fidgeting with the clasp on his overalls.

"The home part. You do have a home as long as you want it," Junior replied.

Tyler frowned, confused by what Junior was telling him. "I'm not following what you're saying, Junior. How can I have a home?"

"Come back to where I live with me, Tyler."

"I can't go in any roofed structure I wasn't in before in life," Tyler countered.

Junior nodded, considering. He remembered something about Barney and Esther. They'd never lived in his home, but they were connected to him. "But don't you see, you already have? You've been in there time and time again."

Tyler shook his head. "I don't understand? How?"

Junior pointed to his chest. "In my heart. You're part of me, so please come home."

Tyler watched his friend for a moment, then nodded with a grin. "Are you sure?"

"More sure than I have been about anything in my life."

EPILOGUE

"Do you remember now?" The old woman's voice was soft and insistent as the pair wandered through the forest hand in hand.

She did. As the building crumbled around her, Magpie remembered everything. How she'd killed her grandpa when he tried to sacrifice her to bring forth every haint in hell. How she'd been locked away in the institution, and the spirits would torment her at night. How, eventually, orderlies came in one night and shocked her with electrodes until she could no longer breathe and felt her soul leave her body.

After that, it got blurry.

"I remember up to when I died, I don't remember anything after that."

Margaret smiled down at her great-granddaughter. "Let me tell you a story about two boys. My sons. One was born strong and stubborn. He wanted to be revered by all. The other was born weak but kind, his body defying him. A truly beautiful soul. I suppose my attention was often on him, and the other boy, your grandfather, became very jealous of that attention. He told the school I couldn't care for my boy Christopher, the gentle one. They took him away. To that place. Uyaga. There he died. I tried to get him out, to bring him home, but they would barely even let me see him. I would visit when they let me, but it was always cut short. I wanted to die with him. After he died, I tried to forget that place, but it called to me."

"You went back?" Magpie asked.

"I did for a while to try and protect the other children, but I couldn't stop the evil forces harming them. I tried telling the authorities, however no one would believe me. The people at Uyaga turned me away because of that. Until they sent you there. Then, I couldn't not go back and it had been enough years, they'd forgotten who I was. I couldn't let another child be consumed by the darkness of that place. You were special. Defiant and pure. Like my sweet boy. Except you were strong and could fight back. Again, my other boy became jealous of your abilities and wanted them for his own. He tried to take them, but you fought. They sent you away, and I followed. The people there weren't the same as before, it had been too many years between and the staff had turned over many times. However, I started to feel the eyes of hell on me. I knew I needed to save you, to get you out of there. They got to you first."

"I remember that part," Magpie whispered.

"When they stole the breath from your body, I decided it wouldn't end unless I ended it. I failed again, though. However, you didn't."

"What happened to Christopher? Is he free?"

Margaret smiled and pointed down the trail to where a teenage boy was waiting for them. "See for yourself."

Magpie squinted and recognized the teenager as the boy from the file at the institution. Except without the marks of suffering. Christopher. He was indeed free.

In every way imaginable.

"So, is it finally over, now?" Magpie asked. "We stopped the evil?"

Margaret sighed and shook her head. "No, honey, we can never end evil. Like the sun in the sky and rivers that flow, it is and will always be. However, we ended that place and the hold it had on those souls. Eventually, it will find a new place, new souls to torment. For now, we can rest and know the ghosts of those souls are now free. We are now free."

Even though Magpie was glad for that, something in her said they'd missed something. One final task left undone, but she couldn't put a finger on it. It sat at the edge of her mind like a shadow. There, but not there. Maybe it would make itself known in time. She squeezed Margaret's hand, and they continued their gentle walk through the quiet forest. Two souls connected in life, now connected in spirit. They were joined by Christopher on the way and strolled together as a family into the forest.

What they didn't see was another spirit, once connected to all three of them, now in a different form, watching from the darkest part of the woods.

Craig's soul had been cast out of his spiritual form by a jealous young, then angry old, man, who wouldn't rest until he got what he wanted. Who was willing to do whatever it took to remain on top. Craig, as he was, no longer existed in body or soul, now vapor in limbo, caught by the action his hands committed but his soul did not.

His wisp of existence no more.

The form of Craig, but the soul of the old man, watched his three family members wander away together, and he swore he would destroy his mother, brother, and granddaughter once and for all. They'd denied him his rightful place between both worlds, and he could never forgive them. He wanted them to pay for their lack of loyalty to him.

Only in making them cease to exist in any form would he get what he believed he deserved. He'd make them regret ever challenging him.

Then, he would be able rule the living and the dead for eternity. To be what he always knew he was. A god.

Close your eyes, get a surprise...

ACKNOWLEDGEMENTS

Thank you to my beta readers:

Shaina Mangum
Mehar Danielle
John Pape
Stephanie Huddle
Brýn Grover
Alyssa Kline
Wayne Turmel
Bruce Baresel
Kati Chastain
Chandra Marie

As always, thank you to my family for supporting me and encouraging me to give life to the voices in my head!

To my readers, you make the story complete.

For my mother, Louise, you taught me to see the spooky side, while remembering the heart comes first.

BOOKS BY JULIET ROSE

Do Over
We Don't Matter
Prick of the Needle
Trigger Point
Through the Surface
Carrying the Dead
Catch the Earth
In Dreams, We Fly
Stitched Together
By the Dimming Light
Expectation of Pain
Done.
Unquiet Forest

***

Anthologies:
Summer Slasher
Books of Horror
Final Passenger
Devour the Rich